# PRAISE FOR BETH KEPHART

### The Great Upending

"Further plot twists lead to an unexpected ending, which readers who love good storytelling and spirited heroines will find satisfying. . . Kephart's latest is ultimately as refreshing as rainfall on a dry field." —*Booklist* Starred Review

### Wild Blues

"Lizzie's story of friendship and family is also one of literary depth; readers will be entranced by this exceptional offering from National Book Award–finalist Kephart."
—*Publishers Weekly* Starred Review

### This Is the Story of You

"A moving epic of a superstorm and how it unravels the lives of those caught in the midst." —*VOYA Ten*

### Going Over

"The language and vivid imagery are exquisite. Smells, sounds and colors pop off the page while the dark barbwired wall (and the Stassi who patrol it) hovers menacingly."
—Parents' Choice Awards, Gold Medal, Historical Fiction

### Small Damages

"[Kenzie's] percolating story emerges through Kephart's lilting prose in the same hazy way you'd meander through the narrow white streets of Seville. . . The reader is lost and found and lost and found again." —*The New York Times Book Review*

# CLOUD HOPPER

National Book Award Finalist **BETH KEPHART**

PENELOPE EDITIONS

PENELOPE EDITIONS is an imprint of Penny Candy Books
Young adult & middle grade books with guts & vision
www.penelopeeditions.com
Oklahoma City & Greensboro

 This book is printed on paper certified to the environmental and social standards of the Forest Stewardship Council™ (FSC®).

Photo of Beth Kephart: William Sulit
Engraving of Sophie Blanchard: Luigi Rados, 1811 (public domain)
Design & cover illustration: Shanna Compton

**Library of Congress Cataloging-in-Publication Data**

Names: Kephart, Beth, author. | Sulit, William, illustrator.
Title: Cloud hopper / Beth Kephart ; with illustrations by William Sulit.
Description: Oklahoma City : Penelope Editions, 2020. | Audience: Ages
   11-14. | Audience: Grades 7-9. | Summary: Fourteen-year-old Sophie and
   her best friends Wyatt and K set out to help when a silent, mysterious
   girl in a homemade hot air balloon lands in rural Gilbertine.
Identifiers: LCCN 2020003972 | ISBN 9781734225907 (hardcover)
Subjects: CYAC: Friendship--Fiction. | Grandmothers--Fiction. |
   Balloonists--Fiction. | Mystery and detective stories.
Classification: LCC PZ7.K438 Clo 2020 | DDC [Fic]--dc23
LC record available at https://lccn.loc.gov/2020003972

24  23  22  21  20     1  2  3  4  5

*For Bill and Jeremy, my forever home, and for Karen Grencik, who offers shelter from the storm*

# PART ONE

# ONE

EVERYONE HAS A NAME, and I have a name, but what I have, which is extra, is a namesake.

*Sophie Blanchard.*

The amazing Sophie Blanchard. One of the greatest lady balloonists who ever puffed up into the sky and flew.

"Aeronaut of the Official Festivals," according to Napoleon Bonaparte.

"Official Aeronaut of the Restoration," according to King Louis XVIII.

"Almighty goddess," according to Grandma Aubrey, who is *my* Grandma Aubrey—the one who gave me my namesake name. *I will call you Sophie B.*

I'm in Gilbertine, which is miles of lovely, farm and sky, latitude and longitude, clean breathing. I'm here in this moment with K and Wyatt. In the grass with the ants and the crickets in the dew, after the best meteor show of the season.

Up above a girl is walking on the clouds. We're watching from down below.

"You think she sees us?" K says.

"Grass is so tall," I say. "And she is so high."

"Doesn't mean that she can't see us," K says.

"No," Wyatt says, sticking a spoon into the jar of her blueberry jam. It's been a good summer for blueberries. "Doesn't mean it, factually."

It's the end of the night and the start of the day in Gilbertine. It's August, and all the beauty's got us whipped. There are miles and miles of atmosphere, and there our cloud hopper goes, her patchwork balloon rising above her head like a giant thought bubble. Her cylinders of fuel are strapped into a pack on her back. Her Doc Martens are a patent-leather pink. Her skirt is a white drip. With her hello hand she works the blast valve and rises. Cruises through a bunch of swallows.

She turns. Does that bouncy thing, touching her boots to the tops of trees, the shingles of roofs, the puffs of clouds. We don't know who she is or where she's come from, but she's ours and so is the show at the start of this day, which is a day when Joseph doesn't need us at the Muni.

You ever seen a hopper?

"Make a wish," Wyatt says. She takes another scrape of sweet fruit from her jar.

We think.

"So?" she wants to know.

"Wishing for diamonds to fall out of the sky," K says, like that's an *of course*, something that anyone would wish for.

Wyatt starts to laugh, the kind of laugh she has trouble stopping.

"Sophie?" she asks, after a minute.

"Wishing on big beauty," I confess.

"You'd know it when you'd see it?"

"Would."

"Hmmm."

"You?"

Wyatt takes a minute. Laughs. "Nobody," she says, "rats out their own wish."

I shrug.

K shrugs.

Bugs buzz.

"You're the extreme worst, Wyatt," I tell her.

The grass is tall around us. Behind us is the Muni— the Quonset huts and the tower, the MIA flags and the taxiway, the Harley coming up the drive and the planes starting to rev. Over the other way is the forest that nobody ever cut down; it just stands there. Wyatt keeps scraping the jam from her jar, and K pillows his head with his Frank Sinatra hat, and I watch the hopper making magic—wobbling and dropping and rising. It's the lines that she pulls that take her up and down into the currents. It's the fuel in her pack that she burns. It's the air of Gilbertine that holds her high as she turns the pink of the dawn into the blue of the day, and now here comes a little puff of gray, not much of anything, out on the horizon.

The facts on us:

K came to Gilbertine by way of a lime-green Gremlin and a mother who says that someday she'll be back. He lost most of his name along the way, so that the K is what's leftover. He lost a lot of stuff, if you want to know the truth, and he sleeps, when he sleeps, inside the ruins of a Skyhawk at the Muni, and he doesn't have much of a namesake, not really. Just that one piece of the alphabet.

Wyatt came by way of a tragedy. We don't talk about it because she won't talk about it. What I know for sure is that she's as good as adopted by Joseph

Bell, who everybody calls the Master of the Muni, because this is his little airport, his land of planes, his Air Time, which is the big balloon operation he runs out of the east end of the hangar.

I came by way of Grandma Aubrey in a Chevy Silverado pickup truck we'd packed thick with stuff. I came from five hundred and four miles south and a touch west one solid year ago, almost to this minute. We drove down and up the Blue Ridge, in and out of the Smokies all to get to Gilbertine, a place we'd found in one of those family scrapbooks that had been tossed in through the short door of Grandma Aubrey's Little Free Library. *Sky for miles and the sky in circles*, someone had written in a caption beneath a crinkling photograph of a beautiful floater.

"I want to wake up to balloons," Grandma Aubrey had said. "Big balloons. I want every day to be a party."

Who needs a mother when you've got a grandmother like mine? I am descendant of the best there is, with a name that's holy bold. My mother left when I was born. Just got up from the birthing bed and vanished, and who needs a mother like that?

Up and down and over we drove, past the hills and around the hills. We drove until we got to Gilbertine where the colors are kale, bread crust, and plum. There are donkeys in the backyards, goats in circles, girls on roller skates, and I don't mean rollerblades, either. We crossed the border when the night was coming on—cantaloupe skies and silhouettes of corn stalks. Grandma Aubrey steered the truck off the road into the back end of a farm and turned the key.

I climbed down from my side and helped her climb down from her side. We hobbled around to the pickup's back end. I gave her a hand and a good push. I jumped up and scuttled ahead and moved the books out of the way, the chalkboards, the suitcases, the bags. We picked our way to the swan-footed couch, and we plopped down, and we sat watching the cantaloupe sky sink and the purple sky rise and the dark go darker.

The stars punching in like peepholes.

I pressed my ear against the shoulder of Grandma Aubrey's shirt.

"You okay?" I asked her.

"Could not be better," she said.

In Gilbertine on that first night, we watched the darkness fall over the grass and the stalks and the cows. We heard the bugs and the birds and the stars crack in. I thought about how far we'd come and how you never really know where you are going and all the lines you cross when you are traveling. Then I wondered if that would be a Sophie Blanchard thought, and I wasn't really sure, so I stopped thinking.

"Storm on the horizon," K says now, breaking into my remembering. He's holding his little finger up to catch the front-end of the weather.

Wyatt turns to see what K's seen.

"Maybe," she says, lines in her brow. "Could be."

She props herself up on her elbow for a better look, and K and I do too. We squint at the sky, watch the farthest horizon. It's like a black horse coming in from another country's distance. A black horse arriving on the bluest day.

"You feel a breeze?" K says.

"I think I do."

"You think the hopper feels the—"

"Sure as hell hope so," K says, and we switch our attention from the black cloud to the hopper—her pink shoes, her patchwork envelope, her feet running on the tops of things. We stare, shielding our eyes from the sun.

"Could be nothing," I say.

"Isn't nothing," K says.

"She probably sees—"

"She'd have to see—"

"She's not coming down. Is she?"

"She *should* come down. Won't she?"

"She has to," Wyatt interrupts us now. "Doesn't she?"

The black horse on the horizon is thundering. The blue sky is getting crowded. There was sun, and now there's not, and it's amazing how fast this storm is running; that's what it feels like: this storm is running. There was nothing, zero, a sunny day. And now there's a storm, and it's running, and we're all three off our backs, standing, looking up, Wyatt with all her gold studs gleaming and K with his Frank Sinatra hat, his black-mop hair curling.

"She's got to come down," he says.

"In a hurry," I say.

"Hey," Wyatt cups her mouth and shouts. "Hey!" Like the hopper could hear her.

"Hey!" K starts shouting too, waving his arms, waving his hat, until we're all jumping, swooshing our arms above our heads, and there's wind in our hair, and the sky's going from one color to another color. Half blue. Half black.

The hopper stays afloat.

The sky is getting worse.

"No," K says. "No!" He shouts.

The first rain falls. A big fat splat.

"She's not coming down," Wyatt says.

"Maybe she can't," I say.

"Maybe something's broken?"

"Broken?"

"Lightning's coming."

"Thunder."

K hates thunder. For a tall guy with muscles living at a Muni, it's insane how much K hates thunder, but there's thunder, and the rain falls, and now it's falling harder. There is a cut of yellow, a little lightning tease. Far away but getting closer.

We're out in the field, no roof over our heads. We scream, we shout, the sky breaks all of a sudden and very bad, and we're running. Through the grass to the Muni drive, the pebbles beneath us crunching. The hangars come in and out of view, the tarmac and the taxiways. We head for the concrete stack of the observation tower, run the curve of the drive, Wyatt up ahead, then K, then me, and when we reach the tower, we climb the outside ladder up and bang open the door and rush straight in. It's old as the Vietnam

War in here—everything frozen in time, rusty and dusty, our favorite hangout. Now it's just the safest place to be to watch the storm and the hopper, the sky still blackening and the wind much worse and the rain so fat, and she's up there, not coming down.

Wyatt picks up the rotary phone on the rusted metal desk and turns her back on the window to protect herself from seeing what she knows will happen next.

"Joseph," she says, into the phone. "The hopper's up. She's still flying."

"I know," Wyatt says.

"That's what I'm saying," Wyatt says.

"I don't know," Wyatt says. "Yes. Exactly."

"Oh my God," K says, and Wyatt turns to watch through the glass.

The storm is on top of the hopper now.

It's dark rain.

It's darkness gusting.

I'm supposed to be as brave as Sophie Blanchard.

Not even.

# TWO

WE SEE THE WHITE DRIP OF HER SKIRT, the pink of her Doc Martens, the patchwork of her hopper-balloon bobbing. We see her scratching the blackness. We see the wind and the trees on the edge of things. We see her bobbing and weaving.

We can't stop an inch of it.

Her legs are cycling the air, desperate for something to catch her. Her skirt is blowing. She's headed for the trees, the trees, the trees, and now the balloon goes pop, and she's falling out of the sky into the tangle of the forest.

"Mayday!" Wyatt shouts now, like she is up there, coming down. "Mayday Mayday!" Into the phone and then to us and now "911, Joseph, 911," and we're out the tower door, down the ladder, running. Toward the ridge of trees, K up in front. We are muddy, gooped, hoping the lightning doesn't strike us. The big black horse of a cloud pours out its heart. We can barely see, and we're still running.

We reach the edge of the forest, the trees thick as ticks. We smack past brambles and old pines and the long barky stems of tulip trees. Beneath our feet we hear the soft pops of pine cones. In another part of the forest we hear Joseph and now Sam and now Everest running in from the other side of the Muni, calling—*hello, hello we're coming*—and when the rain falls now it hits the top of the trees and slides and flops and then knocks these real fat raindrops free, and I wish I'd worn a cap because sometimes I can't see, and if the hopper is hello-ing back I do not hear her.

Does anybody hear her?

Is she talking?

Can she?

Wyatt to the left of me. K to the right, we're running zigzag past the champagne bottles hanging from the trees, the old sheets and the shirts, like somebody's been living out here, like somebody else should be out here helping, and all of us are calling now, shouting out—*Where are you? We're coming. Answer us. Please.* And now someone whistles and everything stops, and K says, "They must have found her," and I say, "I hope somebody found her," and Wyatt says, "No, if they found her we would have heard them shouting that they found her," and Wyatt's out in front, and now K and I are right behind Wyatt into the thickest part of the thick trees, ducking and swatting the limbs out of our way like they are people in a crowd.

Crow call. Rain plink. The sounds of the vets coming up from the other side of the Muni, and Wyatt veers off and we are after her, the sound of her combat boots on the pop of cones, the sound of her yellow skirt swishing, and I can see a sudden clearing where there is only the start of trees and a creek that might have been a dry wide V in the ground if it hadn't been raining. Wyatt jumps the creek, and K and I splash in side by side, bugs stuck to the rain on our faces, and I can hardly breathe.

"K!" Wyatt calls. "Sophie B!"

We are out of breath. We pick up speed.

Up ahead Wyatt has stopped. Just stopped. The long side of her black hair washes to the ground, and there, at her feet, she is: the white skirt, the punched balloon, the pink Doc Martens of the hopper.

Her legs are twisted sticks.

Her arm is bright with blood.

Her eyes are open. Big brown saucer eyes.

K reaches to straighten one leg. Wyatt stops him. Wyatt cups one hand beneath the hopper's head to give her head a little pillow, a little break from the ground she has crashed down on, and whispers soft into her ear:

"We've got you."

And there is so much pain in her face, so much fear that I want to stop and hug her. Hug Wyatt.

The twisted sticks of the legs of the hopper. The big brown eyes in the sweet dark head and one of those eyes inside a swelling of purple, one of those eyes, big as it is, swelling shut, and she closes both eyes now, the celebrity of our sky, this hopper we'd been watching.

The long part of Wyatt's hair streams. Her eyes are—I can't explain them.

There's something she's not saying.

"Tell them we've got her," Wyatt says to K now. "Tell them north, past the stream. Tell them to tell the ambulance team." I reach for the hopper's best hand and hold it, feel her soft grip in mine, and now

Wyatt hums a Spanish song, and I think about K and his wish and the day that started blue, and the rain keeps falling from the trees, but the black cloud has thundered on.

"She's alive," Wyatt says now. "So far."

Past the smash of the hopper's bones, there is the stuff of her hopping machine, all that has been shattered in the forest. Rusty parts of rusted things. The patchwork balloon with its busted crooked seams.

"Not usual," Wyatt says, looking too.

"No," I say.

"From one of the farms?" Wyatt says, meaning the fields of Gilbertine where the migrants work, especially now, in August.

"But how could that be?" I say. "How would that work? How would a mushroom picker's daughter get a hopper? A tomato picker's daughter? A strawberry picker's daughter? An apple picker's?"

"Right," she says. "Exactly."

"Doesn't seem like—"

"Who are you?" Wyatt whispers to the girl. "What's your name?" Her voice so soft that the girl with her head in Wyatt's palm, her hand in my hand, her body on the forest floor, broken in a thousand directions, might not hear her. "Where did you come from? Why didn't you stop for the storm?"

There're gnats at our heads. Blood suckers. The crows that had been higher in the forest trees have flapped down to a closer branch. Straining their heads to see.

"Mind your own," Wyatt says, looking up, and then she looks down again, and the girl is barely breathing, and both her eyes are closed.

We can hear the men running. We can hear Sam's voice on the phone, and now I see them—Everest in his 'Nam jacket with the medals pinned on, the red shirt beneath that, and Joseph in his silver Air Time jacket and his pilot's cap, and Sam in his green windbreaker—the old pilots and their rescue mission in the woods.

"Damn it," Joseph says, when he reaches the girl. Shakes his head. Angry, now wordless.

"Yeah," Wyatt says, and now it's Everest, kneeling close, saying, "We have to get her out of here. No time to lose."

"Don't move her."

"She's bleeding out."

"Ambulance is coming." Sam says.

"Needs a tourniquet," Everest says, and now he's ripping his jacket off, also the sleeves from his shirt. He is lifting the hopper's arm. He is tying.

"You'll be okay," Wyatt whispers. "Tell us your name."

# THREE

"HEY," I SAY TO WYATT. "Hey."

We're watching Gilbertine rush past in Joseph's truck, Joseph and Sam up front, K and me on either side of Wyatt in the back, our arms around her.

She won't stop crying. Joseph's jammed into fastest gear behind the ambulance. Everest is up there, with the sirens and the girl, and we're passing the cows and the chickens and the barns and the silos. We've left the Quonset hangars behind us, like half-moons on the horizon.

Sun is coming back now.

The black-horse cloud is gone.

Wyatt is a waterworks.

"Hey," I say again.

K gives her shoulders a squeeze, the two of them like brother and sister, the three of us like family, because all of us live in the same house, or kind of.

Or all of us will, someday, according to Grandma Aubrey, who asks me to be brave.

No radio on. Nobody guessing who the hopper is or why she wouldn't stop flying or if she's going to make it. She has to make it. She was the star of our summertime show. She was a part of us, and she didn't even know it.

Joseph brakes fast at Gilbertine Medical. Parks. We jump out, see Everest following the gurney into the hospital, his jacket back on to hide his torn-up red shirt. By the time we get inside, the hopper is being whisked down the hall; she's getting smaller and smaller. Two big doors swing open. They swing closed.

"Better," Sam says, "to wait here."

# FOUR

I DITCH MY SCHWINN at the side of the house, the front wheel up like a horse in buck. I take the porch steps two at a time, ease the screen door behind me. The storm is long gone. The sky is pure blue.

"That you, Sophie?" Grandma Aubrey says.

"Yeah."

"News?"

"They still have her in Trauma."

I'd called, so Grandma Aubrey would know. I'd told her I'd get home soon as we knew more than we did. We don't know more. They sent us back to the Muni, and I grabbed my bike and I rode and I'm here, everything hurting and lungs out of breath.

Wyatt said she needed space. Said, "Sophie, go on home."

K said nothing. K walked the tunnel between the planes and slammed into his Skyhawk, and then he turned and looked at me, and I looked into the skies of his eyes, and I wanted to ask him—anything. Wanted to stay until he said something good, like, "Nothing to worry about, Sophie B," but K—he might not talk much, but he's definitely no liar. He'll choose silence every time over the untrue thing.

Grandma Aubrey's propped up on her bed. The windows are open like, in any kind of weather, she loves them to be open—let the bugs in, let the wind, let all the rain that fell, puddles on the floor. The things I hung from the ceiling by strings when we first moved in are swooping in the breeze—the origami birds flying, the papier-mâché balloons bobbing, the star maps riffling. Grandma Aubrey's bed is white. Her sheets are white. Her hair is white. She's wearing one of her white oxfords. Across the room, like a wall of bricks, are the books we have no shelves for, the stacks of newspapers we will never throw away. Take one book out, one headline, and the rest could fall.

"Got Wyatt's latest cook," I say, trying to brighten the hour, trying to keep my own grandma from worrying, because this is what worries her worst of all, her not being able to do much of anything for me, for K, for Wyatt, now for this girl who fell from the sky. She's sick, and when you're sick, the sick takes over. Multiple sclerosis is mean like that. It's a very mean disease.

"You'll thank her?" Grandma Aubrey says, meaning Wyatt.

"Already did," I say, letting the silence fill in. Giving us both room to watch the window and think our thoughts, then I can't help it. I spill.

"It's bad," I say. "It's really bad with the hopper."

"Oh, honey."

"The storm was coming, and she kept flying."

"A bad mistake," she says. "With consequences."

"Don't know if it was a mistake. Don't know anything, actually."

"They have a name for her?"

"No."

"They have anyone who's come to see her?"

"Not yet."

"You got her where she . . . needs to be," Grandma Aubrey says, taking another extra breath, MS being a breath stealer of a disease. "You did what you could."

The words don't make either one of us feel better.

I pull my own jar of Wyatt's blueberry jam out of the deepest pocket of my pale pink hoodie jacket. I snag a Ziploc bag of saltine crackers from another. I pop the knife out of my Swiss contraption and make a jam-a-lade and cracker sandwich. Go to the kitchen to get some water. Pass it on.

Grandma Aubrey takes a bite, littlest mouse bite of a bite. She closes her eyes, chews, swallows. When she opens her eyes they're more blue than they'd been.

"That child," she says, "is pure genius."

"Yeah," I say.

"The sensitive type."

"Funny," I say. "Funny sensitive."

"You remember our . . . first time," Grandma Aubrey says, "when we met Wyatt?"

"Yeah."

"You remember the first time you tasted one of her blues?"

"Who'd forget it?"

"Girl seemed like she was the mayor of Gilbertine. Like nothing bad could happen if she was living here."

"This is bad," I say. "With the hopper."

I sit on the edge of the bed beside Grandma Aubrey. I think back to how it was—our first morning in Gilbertine after the night of our coming. Grandma

Aubrey and I were in hard need of the Ladies, and there was that diner, the Twenty Four, blinking its ALL NIGHT. ALL WELCOME. sign. There were horses in the parking lot, a bunch of Harleys, a couple of Schwinns, two men beneath straw hats speaking Spanish. I got us both through the door and into the bathroom and into the stalls, then to the sinks. I ran my hands through my long hair. Grandma kept hers Einstein-style.

Next we made our way past the red booths to the red stools. We climbed up. We caught our balance. There was Wyatt with her vertical worry line beneath a fringe of black punk rock hair, long hair on right side, bristles on the left. There was a mean scar on her wrist that ran up her arm, high as her quarter sleeve. There were earrings everywhere and blueberry pies behind the counter glass.

"Two slices, please," Grandma Aubrey said. "One for each."

Wyatt smiled.

"Make that four. Two each."

Wyatt touched the fifteen square gold posts in her right ear, one for each year she'd been alive. She touched the bright round hoop that dangled from her left ear, the tiny cross in her nose, then pulled out the pie.

"We're two southern girls," Grandma Aubrey said, juicing up her accent for effect. "North Carolina."

"And you came all this way for pie?"

"Five hundred miles," I said. "Or so."

"Heard there were floaters here," Grandma Aubrey said.

"Floaters," Wyatt repeated.

"The big balloons," Grandma Aubrey said. "Of Gilbertine."

"*Sky in circles*," I repeated the scrapbook promise. "*Sky for miles*." Not mentioning my name or the reason for our interest. You don't just start talking about the great female aeronaut Sophie Blanchard to a stranger in a diner. Not everybody knows the name, even if they should.

"So you didn't drive all that way for pie," Wyatt said.

"Your pie's a bonus," Grandma Aubrey said, because by now Wyatt had cut us each our two slices and put them on plates and handed us the forks.

"We're planning on living here," Grandma Aubrey said, after she was finished, her fork scraping the blue juice off the plate.

"Well. That's a surprise. Hardly anybody ever moves to Gilbertine."

"We're hardly hardly anybody."

Wyatt gave us a look. She smiled. "The big balloon flies out of Air Time," she said. "Air Time runs out of the Muni. You get settled. You come back. I'll make the introductions."

"We shall be taking you up on your offer," Grandma Aubrey said, a dot of pie on her chin. I cleaned her off with a diner napkin. Grandma Aubrey paid, going extra on the tip. I helped her from the stool. We waved goodbye. In a couple of days we came back.

Wyatt talked.

The Muni, she told us, is where she lives. Actually, factually, she said, she lives in a house on the edge of the airport with Joseph Bell. Instead of a yard, she has a blueberry farm that she calls Hope, and instead of a garage she has a factory, and in that factory she bakes her blues. Every single berry treat that she makes is factory-made, including her blueberry pie. Saturday mornings she has the diner job, which is as good as a laboratory for testing the effects of her blues on paying customers.

Market research, Wyatt said.

*Market research.*

I sit here remembering. I sit here until Grandma Aubrey falls asleep. She is snoring like she does, her air getting caught in her throat. I lean back into the mound of pillows that bloom beside her head. I hear the click of the nails of Harvey the fat cat coming. I hear him jump. I feel his soft paws by my head. I see the first time I ever saw the Muni of Gilbertine, the first time I ever saw K, the first time I ever saw the big Hot Air go up, the first time I ever helped—laying the big tarp across the grass, flapping it down like a picnic cloth, wrangling the balloon out of its bag and drawing it out across the tarp beneath the night that was becoming the dawn while the men checked the inflator fan, and Everest checked the lines, and Joseph tossed the pibal to the sky—and I try to keep my recent history filming past, but I stumble over thoughts about the hopper: The line of blood on her arm. The smash of her legs, her broken machine, her eyes swelling shut, the doctor saying to Joseph, when he had finally come out, that he'd never seen a case like this, a case so complicated. Wyatt had pounded one fist into her thigh, touched the cross pricking her nose.

"Not good enough," she'd said.

"Wyatt," Joseph said. "Let the doctors do their work." He was still wearing his silver Air Time jacket and his rain-soaked pilot's cap and his turnip nose and his little ears and his dog tags on a chain.

"We need more information," Wyatt said.

She paced. She wouldn't sit. She went up and down the hall talking to anyone wearing a name badge. "Somebody's gotta be looking for her," she kept saying. "Waiting for her. Worrying. Somebody needs to get told."

But nobody had called about a missing hopper.

# FIVE

EARLY, THE SUN JUST OUT, I Schwinn the yellow
lines of the empty road between the cottage and the
Muni, then spin up the drive. I brake at the huts, prop
my bike, head through the glass door. The lounge is
cushion chairs and relic sofas and an abandoned welcome desk. The whiteboard on the wall advertises the
price of fuel. Jason and Mikey, two old geezers who
are always here, don't look up and don't stop talking,
something about rolling in toast and tail dragger
crashes, the hammerhead maneuvers that turned the
belly of a Cobra to the sky. Now they're arguing plane
porpoising and poor flying and frog fog, and one of
them says that somebody should have mentioned the
cost of a new tug.

Behind them, on the TV, the news is on, volume
down, closed caption reading: *Unidentified teen falls
from the sky.*

The camera pans over the forest. The camera reels in close. Now it's not the forest but the Muni and now not the Muni but Everest in a white shirt beneath the leather jacket, his 'Nam medals shining.

"Turn it up," I say. "Mikey?"

But by the time they notice what's on the screen and find the remote the story's gone.

"That was Everest," I say. "Talking."

"A regular celebrity," Mikey says, shaking his head.

"On the *TV*," I say.

"Crew came up yesterday," Jason says. "Late. Joseph said he wouldn't talk, and Sam's Sam, so it boiled down to Everest."

"Speak of the devil," Jason says.

"Devil?" Everest says, behind me, and I turn. "Since when?" He'll always be the tallest old fighter pilot of the Muni. I'm not so short, but my head tilts up.

"You were on TV?" I say.

"I guess that's right."

"What'd they want to know?"

"What you'd expect. How she fell, where she fell, who she is. Only got two of the three. Only got one of them, precisely. How she fell is also, at this time, a mystery."

His eyes are like two pieces of sky on a good sky day. One of them is freckled. I think about a family out there, watching the news. *Unidentified teen falls from the sky.* I think about Everest being the spokesperson for the tragedy. He was probably handsome once. He probably never knew it.

"How she fell is she fell," I say.

"The question is what failed? The question is why was she flying in the first place? Accident? Intentional? Police have been out there, combing the site. Thing was the strangest thing. Some of it pure machine. Some of it jury-rigged."

"You were there? With the police?"

"I was escorting. Me and Sam."

"Did they have anything? The police? On her, I mean."

"Not that anybody's telling me."

"Any news from Trauma?"

"Joseph's called. Status quo, is what they told him."

"That's it?"

"It," he says.

"Wyatt around?" I ask.

"Saw her somewhere," he says. He nods in the direction of the Pop-Tarts, the PayDays, the sloppy bowl of Chef Boyardee on top of the microwave. I head off, past the folding cots, the rolled-up blanket, and now I stare down into the belly of the hangar, the long tunnel of Pipers, Cessnas, Taylorcrafts, WACOs, planes with their names painted on, their numbers, one plane stripped to the bones like a dinosaur in a natural history museum.

The light coming in through a band of windows holds the floating bits of dust in place. There are barn swallows in the high parts, and the air is thick and greasy. Smells like fuel and mouse poop and cut grass, and down there, at the end of the line, is K's Skyhawk, where he lives. I think of the first time I saw him there, the first time I tried to imagine if it's lonely or peaceful sleeping inside a pair of wings.

"But what was she like?" I sometimes ask K, about his mom.

"Full of shine," K will say. But that's it. K's lost more than his name, or maybe he hasn't lost it. Maybe he's just really good at hiding what is his.

"Hey."

I turn. It's Wyatt wearing a strawberry-colored shirt and a puff of flour on her collar, a pair of jeans tucked into her high yellow boots. She has the smell of blueberries on her and a couple of birds hopping around at her feet.

"Hey," I say.

"Everest was on TV," I say.

"Local hero," she says. "You coming?"

She starts walking.

I'm walking.

"Grandma Aubrey loved the jam-a-lade," I say.

"Yeah," she says.

We keep walking.

Through the cool height of the hangar. Past the hoses and the wrecker truck. From the west end of the hangar huts to the east end, Air Time, where the big balloon lives.

Wyatt stops to write something down. She tears the page in half and files it inside a rusty drawer. Now we head through the parasail door that opens to mowed grass and then a fence and beyond the fence the Bluejays and the Ivanhoes of the farm she calls Hope. Two hundred blueberry bushes all dug in, each bush with some history to it and a name written down on a Popsicle stick. Past the bushes, on the long clothesline, Wyatt's got her white sheets hung, and past the sheets is the square house that is Wyatt's house, which is Joseph Bell's house too. And next to that is the factory.

"I've been busy," Wyatt says, not like she has to.

"Yeah," I say.

"Stuff to do," she says.

"What stuff?"

"Harnessing the power of persuasion."

I wait.

She doesn't complete the sentence. If that is a sentence.

On the runway, on the other side of the hangar, a prop plane is whipping itself up into a noisy frenzy. The factory door is stuck open with a brick. We step up into the gleam. The stainless machines and twin porcelain sinks and Mason jars: Wyatt's world. Lemons, limes, garlic on the sill. Pots hanging from ceiling hooks with their copper bottoms scrubbed. On Wyatt's whiteboard the blues are written out:

*Blueberry pizza*
*Blueberry sweet onion salad*

*Blueberry onion-sauced pork*
*Blueberry crumble*
*Blueberry lemon pound cake*
*Blueberry blintze*
*Blueberry salsa*
*Blueberry fool*

A buzzer rings. Wyatt pulls two mitts from the hooks above her head and bends into the steam of her oven. With each gloved hand she snatches a skillet.

"Dutch pancakes," she says.

They look like polka dot balloons.

"Delicious?" I ask.

"You're actually, factually asking?"

"Delicious," I say.

Wyatt never lacks for baking confidence.

She puts the skillets onto the cooling racks.

She pulls the mitts off her hands.

She taps confectioner's sugar through a sifter and makes it snow. She sprinkles extra blueberries over the pancakes, snatches two forks, gives me one.

She pokes the juice out of a berry with the tine of her fork. We scrape the skillets clean.

"I've been fine tuning," she says.

"For the purpose of?"

"We're being gracious."

"Gracious?"

"Ain't a doctor or a nurse on staff who wouldn't appreciate my bakes," she says.

"So?"

"We're heading back to Gilbertine Medical. We're getting news on the hopper."

"Aren't there doctor rules?" I say. "About talking about patients?"

"You have another plan?"

"Nope," I admit. "I have no plan."

"So it's settled."

I see K's shadow falling through the door. I turn. He's wearing his Converse sneakers, those freckles on his face, more on the one side than the other. He grabs a spoon and digs the warm crumbs from the bottom of the skillet.

"Taste testing without me?" he says.

"We're going to see the hopper," Wyatt says.

K's eyes grow big. He looks older than he is but he's actually my age, which is one year younger than Wyatt, a fact she likes to toss around when she has ideas she thinks we'll question. "She's taking visitors?"

"We're taking a round of my blues to Gilbertine.
Mosey around. Look for news."

"Sophie?" K says.

I shrug. "Got nothing better. You?"

"Nothing remotely."

"Precisely," Wyatt says.

# SIX

THE DUTCH ARE IN THE BAKERY BOX. The box is in a basket. The basket is strapped to the rusty handlebars of Wyatt's bike, and Wyatt rides the fastest. The hospital is four miles south from the Muni, down the main road, then down another, past the farms where picking season is in full force, the sound of Spanish songs on the radios, and we're one two three in a row, and K's hat flies off, and he has to turn around to get it.

I'd called Grandma Aubrey from the Muni before we left to ask her how she was. She answered after seven rings.

"Wyatt's been on a bake," I'd said.

"Don't forget," she'd said.

"What?"

"Your manners. Sometimes a short hello . . . is the best hello. Especially with doctors."

We know about doctors, Grandma Aubrey and me. We know too much. We left all of hers in the valley after the last one said, *Live*. That was it. *Live. You only have time for that.*

MS is the meanest mean.

The hospital is the newest thing in Gilbertine. It's not that big. Bricks the color of sand. Trees along the front, their tops cut off. Everything square and one-story simple with a bunch of machines stuck up on the roof, the machines all bright and shiny.

Now out in the parking lot there's a rack for bikes. Wyatt is off hers in a flash. She takes the box out of the basket.

"You ready?" she asks, when K finally wheels in.

"Ready." He straightens his hair beneath the hat he's crushed on harder.

It's K on one side, me on the other, Wyatt in the center with her box. "We're here on behalf of hopper," Wyatt says to the lady at reception, who has owl-eye glasses, big and curious.

"Sounds like a regular delegation," she says, suspicious already.

"Indeed. We'd like to thank the staff for its attentions."

"That right?"

"It is."

"You're Wyatt Bell?" the owl-eye glasses lady says. "Aren't you? You were here with your father yesterday."

"We were all here," Wyatt says. "This is K. This is Sophie. We have a bake."

Wyatt cracks the lid of the box. She lets the warm fumes rise.

"Well," the lady says. "I see."

"Have a taste," Wyatt says.

"Oh no. I couldn't."

"There's plenty," Wyatt says, "to go around."

"Well," the lady says. "If you insist."

"We insist," Wyatt says, pulling a bright knife from her pocket. She opens the lid all the way, slices a nice perfect slice, stands straight, waits.

The owl-eye glasses lady cannot help herself from reaching in. "Oh, my," she says. "Well. Yes."

"On behalf of the hopper," Wyatt repeats herself more definitively, "we would like to thank the staff."

K shifts, foot to foot.

"Well," the lady says. "Can't see the harm in it."

"Can't see it either," K says, and Wyatt elbows him. When you're on the verge of a win, you don't press your advantage.

"Trauma's that way," the lady says. "There's a nursing station. You can leave your—what do you call this?—there."

"Dutch pancakes," Wyatt says, slicing another piece for the lady. "Blueberries straight from my farm."

"*Your* farm?"

"That's right, ma'am, and thank you."

The owl-eye glasses lady's mouth is full. She mumbles and waves. Wyatt closes the lid of the box, and we're headed down to Trauma—through the double doors into the shining light. You'd think we'd walk fast, but we walk slow. We walk three across without saying a word, some heat still in the pancakes.

"Hello," we say to a doctor passing by.

"Morning," he says.

We keep walking.

"Hello," we say to a wheelchair man.

"That's Harry," Wyatt whispers. "Used to order triple eggs at the Twenty Four."

The doors swing open at a simple button touch. The space is doughnut shaped. Rooms in a circle around a circular desk. Rooms with curtains instead of doors. The beeping of machines, some rooms in darkness.

"Can I help you?" a tall guy in blue scrubs asks. He's behind the desk, typing into a computer. He wears a stethoscope instead of a necklace.

"Here on behalf of the hopper," Wyatt says.

He squints up. We're leaning over some partition glass.

"*Cloud* hopper," I say.

"The girl," K says, "who fell."

"You're the family?" the guy asks, full of suspicion for the obvious reason. We don't look like the hopper. She doesn't look like us.

"In a way of speaking," Wyatt says, but I pull her back. There's a difference between lying and persuading.

"We found her," I say, "in the woods."

"We watched her," K says, "in the sky."

"These are Dutch pancakes," Wyatt says. "Made fresh on the farm."

She opens the lid and lifts the box up and over the partition. She hands him her knife. "See what I mean," she says.

"You were here yesterday," he says. "I saw you. Waiting."

We nod. "We're still waiting," Wyatt says, "for news."

"There are rules," the nurse says.

"We are aware," I say.

"We just came to say thanks," K says. "Thanks for taking care of the hopper."

He looks up at us, then down at the box. He lifts the knife. He tastes.

"Wow."

"Wyatt's the baker at the Twenty Four," I say. "You ever been there?"

"I have not."

"This is what you're missing."

"Seems I'm missing quite a lot."

Wyatt shrugs. She waits.

"The hopper's out of surgery," the nurse says. "I can tell you that." He shifts his shoulder, and I see a crooked name badge. YAM, it says, and I wonder if it's short for something.

"She's alive," I say. "In other words."

"Yes," Yam says. "She is."

Wyatt's eyes turn into tears. She hits her cheek with her thumb. A doctor behind a surgical mask passes. A woman pushes through a curtain door, maybe a wife of someone dying. Now another nurse comes by, grabs a chart from the nursing station desk.

She's cool in mint green scrubs. She has a blonde ponytail that starts high on the back of her head. She's underlined her eyes with blue, but her eyes are green. Her name tag says NURSE CARA.

"What's this?" she says.

"They call them Dutch pancakes," Yam says. "I believe. Dutch pancakes. Is that the technical term?"

She turns toward Wyatt. "I've heard of those."

"You have?"

"Heard they sell down at the Twenty Four. Everybody I know says, if you get to the Twenty Four, have the Dutch."

"They're not an everyday menu item," Wyatt says.

"They're not?"

"I rotate the goods," Wyatt says. "I'm in charge of the blues. You ever been to the diner?"

"I have not."

"Come anytime," Wyatt says. "The blues will be on me."

"So you're Wyatt Bell," Nurse Cara says.

"I am."

"Honored," she says, bows a bit. "Your reputation," she says, "precedes you."

Yam hands Nurse Cara the knife. She cuts herself a slice. She closes her eyes, and she chews.

"Wow," she says.

"That's what I said," Yam says. Then: "They're friends with the hopper."

"Friends?" Nurse Cara says.

"Of a sort," K says.

"We were hoping for news," Wyatt says.

Nurse Cara is chewing. She looks at us, at Yam, back at us. "Can't say much," she finally says. "Only that she's out of surgery. She's in recovery."

"She's going to make it," Wyatt says. "Right?"

"She's going to make it," Nurse Cara says. "But getting better will take a very long time."

Yam raises his finger. Nurse Cara stops.

"If you could share the Dutch," Wyatt says, "with her team."

"If you could tell them it's from us—or mostly her," K says, nodding at Wyatt.

"Come back," Nurse Cara says. "Another day."

K removes his hat. He bows.

Somebody taught him manners, I think. Someone. Maybe his mom.

# SEVEN

"So," GRANDMA AUBREY SAYS when I get back. "*So.*"

I find her sitting up against her pillows, watching the world from her bed. She looks like she's just run a marathon, if she could run a marathon, if she ever had. Her hair in tufts, her night shirt off the rack of her shoulders, her face pale as her hair is pale, her fingers limp. Every move is hard on Grandma Aubrey. Waiting's hard. She waits. It's hard.

"You okay?" I ask.

"Could not be better," she says.

Little loving lies.

"Hopper's alive," I say, "and out of surgery."

"Very good," Grandma Aubrey says.

"We met her nurse."

"You met her . . . nurse?"

"Wyatt made a batch of Dutch. We introduced ourselves."

Grandma Aubrey shakes her head. She waits for me to explain, but I can't explain. For me to share news, but there's no more news.

"Harvey been behaving himself?" I finally ask.

"He's been a good-boy cat."

"You hungry?"

"There any more of that jam-a-lade?"

"Coming," I say.

"And ice cream?"

"That too."

"A bowl for Harvey?"

We keep two-gallon tubs on hand. Handel's Vanilla. Butter Brickle. I balance the yellow, blue, and green bowls on top of the tubs, the scoop, the jam, the crackers, two spoons. I go back for the milk and paper towels. It's a bed-blanket picnic, like we do, and we all eat, Harvey too, until we are good and done—and now when Grandma Aubrey closes her eyes I close my eyes and remember the days down south when Grandma Aubrey was still walking with her two canes and teaching weather on the kitchen chalkboard, teaching math, teaching the story of Sophie Blanchard, born Marie Madeline-Sophie Armani Blanchard. *You could say our heroine was afraid of horse carriages and ambulatory rumble, out of kilter with rocks and sand and general planetary topography, made desperate by shoe scuffle,* she'd begin with her story, drawing in a deep breath and talking like she was reading from a book she'd memorized, except they were her own words she remembered, polished, perfected. *You could say that down on earth Sophie Blanchard was afraid and up above—in a basket, beneath the envelope of a swollen silk balloon—she was ablaze. You could say that the earth scorched her feet, but the sky. Oh that sky.*

Sophie Blanchard sailed sixty flights in all. Then, Grandma Aubrey used to say, she came for us—across continents and centuries. *See that, Sophie B,* she'd say, and I was seven or eight or maybe nine, standing at the window in the house down south, with a big storm coming on. The wind would be screaming, and the trees would be bending, and the storm would be blowing blue into the valley, and Grandma Aubrey would hold me close and say, *The world has gone elastic. The sky is an elastic shift.*

That's what she'd say—*elastic shift.* That's how she'd talk, when she was still ahead of the MS, when she was still standing, with her canes, when I wasn't even wondering about what might happen next because we were right there, together, the two of us, no deserting mother needed. She'd point to somewhere beyond the window and ask if I could see what she'd seen: Sophie Blanchard herself with her sky-high balloon perched like a hat above her head, her dress all white and plumed.

I can't see it, I'd say.

And then, one day, I did.

"There," she said, when I told her that. "There. I've taught you everything you need."

Being brave, I think she meant. Being willing to see what other people can't see. Being okay crossing state lines and territories to move to Gilbertine so we could chase the picture of the big balloon we'd found in our Little Free Library. I've never told Wyatt the whole truth. I haven't told K. I figure you can still call two kids your best friends without telling them every last thing.

"Tell me a story," Grandma Aubrey says. Wyatt will call if there is news on her end. Harvey will meow if he needs the door. I rearrange the pillows and begin.

"The history of us," I say.

"You were . . . peach fuzz," she says.

". . . and healthy scream and nothing pretty," I say, using the words she used to say to me. "I was ten toes and ten fingers, and you were the one who was counting," I say. I take her hand into my hand. She stretches out her fingers. She is listening.

"You remember that Grandma Aubrey?" I say.

"Tell it, Sophie," she says.

"There was only one choice when I was born, and you made it."

"I did," she whispers.

"My mother had places to go, but you weren't leaving."

"That's right."

"You went cane by foot by cane by foot down the wide hospital hall. Over the linoleum squares. Around the welcome desk. Through the lobby. And straight through the revolving doors. All the way down the street, to city hall, wearing your green skirt with its elastic waist and your orthopedic shoes and one of your oxfords."

"Yes."

"You opened the door and marched in and said—"

"I have a granddaughter. Named Sophie B. For Sophie Blanchard. Greatest ... aeronaut who ... ever lived."

"That's what you did," I say.

"I did."

"Because my mother had her itchy feet."

"Always did," Grandma Aubrey says.

"And I got lucky," I say.

"No," she says, like she always does. "I did. You're the best thing that ever happened to me, Sophie B."

Behind the lids of her eyes I see the little dreams playing. If I told her more now she would not hear me. If I told her more she wouldn't have to. This is her story, this one that I'm telling. The one that she gave me.

"Time to sleep," I say.

"You know where I'll be when I'm not . . . here anymore?" she says.

"You'll always be here," I say.

"I'll be out there," she said, pointing to the window. "In the yonder. Where you can see me."

"Don't want to talk about it," I say.

"Nothing to be afraid of," she says. "You're my brave . . . Sophie B."

No, I think. No. No. No. Beauty without Grandma Aubrey will never be big.

Sometimes I remember the blue valley and the elastic shift. Sometimes I pretend that Grandma

Aubrey isn't dying. Sometimes I can't believe how unlucky and lucky a person can be at the same time.

"Always room for you at the Muni," Wyatt says, and Joseph Bell and K and Everest and Sam—they say it too. "Always welcome, when you need us."

"Shhh, Grandma Aubrey," I say, her head against my shoulder now, my hand on Harvey's tummy.

"Shhh," to both of us.

# EIGHT

GRANDMA AUBREY IS NO COOK, and I am also no cook, but I do know a few things. I can do hot dogs in a pan, I can heat pizza in the oven, I can put sandwiches on rye, I can put ice cream in a bowl, I can follow the recipe for mac and cheese, and tonight was mac and cheese.

"Well done," Grandma Aubrey had said. Except she'd hardly eaten anything.

The windows are open. The crickets are in chirp. There's a solid half-moon and a bunch of stars, and if I listen through the open breeze of the night I can hear the cows a farm or two down, flicking at the darkness with their tails. A couple of fireflies have zoomed in, snapping when they fly. We turn the lights off so we can watch them light up. Then I catch them and walk to the window and set them free again.

"Might as well," Grandma Aubrey says now, "turn on the TV."

I roll out of her bed and fetch the TV from the floor—an antique box from our home down south. Wyatt wasn't even sure what it was when she saw it sitting there, and K said, *That thing'll never work*, but when I make room for it on the bureau and turn it on and wait, a picture comes in, but on only one channel. *Who needs more than one channel?* Grandma Aubrey says, like she says, *Who needs school when you have books?* Like she says, *Your birth mother will never know the first scintilla of everything she's missing.* My birth mother, who is also Grandma Aubrey's daughter, but she doesn't like to be reminded of that.

It's the end of one show. It's the start of the news. I pick up our plates so I can clean them. I'm soaping the pot when I hear Grandma Aubrey call. "You need," she says, sputtering, "to see this."

It's Gilbertine on the TV screen—the pretty farms, the horse and buggies, the Muni. The camera pans in and out, and now the anchor lady's talking, and now the picture is the hospital where the hopper's out of Trauma. That's what the lady with the smooth hair and the square glasses is saying, calling our girl the girl who fell from the sky, the girl who is a stranger.

"Authorities suspect," she's saying . . .

"No one has come forward," she's saying.

"Please call this tip line."

"How could nobody come forward?" I say, more to the TV than to Grandma Aubrey, more to myself because I do not understand, even for a second, how a girl could fly like that and crash like that and there be nobody rushing to be with her.

Or maybe it's more like I don't want to understand how nobody could be rushing to be with her. Maybe I don't know—except maybe I do—that there are complications here, that whoever steps forward on behalf of the hopper will be asked to give up secrets. Secrets like a name. Secrets like an address. Secrets like papers that might not exist. It's in the newspapers. It's on the TV. The truth depends on which channel you watch, Grandma Aubrey says. The truth and the danger, the fear.

"Speculation continues to grow," the anchor is saying, and now the phone rings, and I pick it up, and it's my best friend in this world if you also count K and Grandma Aubrey.

"You watching this?" she says, and I picture Wyatt at the Muni, in the house behind the factory, the TV on and Joseph beside her.

"Yeah," I say. "I'm watching."

"We're going back," she says.

I nod. She can't see me nod.

"Tomorrow. Get here by six?"

"A.M.?"

"Not waiting all day, Sophie."

I take a long look at Grandma Aubrey, then at Harvey, our good fat guard cat.

"Yeah," I say. "I'll be there."

# NINE

I RIDE THE YELLOW LINE of the road, the dawn fog lifting. The air is heavy with the smell of hay, with gnats that smack against my speed. "I'll be back," I'd whispered in Grandma Aubrey's ear when I was leaving. A glass of orange juice on the bedside table, a bowl of raisins and granola, a bowl of milk for Harvey.

"You be good."

"I'll be good."

"You remember . . ."

". . . manners."

At the Muni, K and Wyatt are waiting out front, their kickstands up, a box strapped to Wyatt's basket, the smell of the cake cutting the smell of sweet hay.

"One extra teaspoon of vanilla extract," Wyatt says. "Makes all the difference." She must have baked away the midnight hour.

She's pedaling, we're pedaling. There's still hardly anybody out except for us and now a horse and buggy and a Harley and that girl on roller skates, and with the sun a little higher over the dawn the farms along the road are coming out of shadow, like somebody pulling back a blanket. There are already workers out there, pickers, the sound of Spanish songs on a wheezy radio.

It's Saturday, and Wyatt should be at the Twenty Four, market researching her latest bake, making her tip money. She must have called in, I think. She must have said *family business*. She must have said *important is important*. And nobody's going to fire Wyatt from the diner.

Privileges for the blueberry genius with the farm called Hope.

Down the road, past the sign, up the drive, we park the bikes. The reception lady with the owl-eye glasses smiles when she sees us. Then she frowns. "You're awfully early," she says.

"Cake's still warm," Wyatt says. "Blueberry cake with vanilla hues."

"*Hues*," the woman says.

Wyatt tips the lid open. Slices in. The knife comes out clean. "First taste?" she offers.

The woman rolls her eyes—*so good, so great*—and chews.

"We know our way," Wyatt says, slicing out another sliver for the lady.

The woman lifts her finger, tries to swallow, but it's too late.

We hurry.

Down the hall. Through the doors. To Trauma.

It's not Yam at the front desk.

It's no one, actually.

It's just us in the center of the doughnut, the circle of rooms in their full circle. The curtains are pulled shut where the doors should be. Machines bleep and they blip. We can see some shoes beneath the curtain. White shoes. Sneakers. Clogs. The clock reads five of seven, and it's K and me, waiting on Wyatt. K in his black T-shirt and Sinatra hat, still looking sleepy despite the bike ride in the fresh air. Wyatt with the blue tips of her fingers. Me with the legs of my jeans rolled so tight nobody will know they're flood pants.

I'm the tallest, Wyatt's the thinnest, K's the strangest: those are facts.

The doors behind us whoosh, they swing apart. It's Nurse Cara, the arms of a sweater tied over her mint green scrubs.

"Well," she says, coming around to her side of the desk and slamming her wide purse onto the back of a chair.

"Cake?" Wyatt asks.

Nurse Cara shakes her head no. Then shakes her head yes. "Why not?" she says.

"The kicker," I say, "is the vanilla extract."

"Good God," Nurse Cara says.

Wyatt shrugs.

"Exactly how old are you?" she asks Wyatt now.

"Fifteen," Wyatt says.

"You've got some future."

"I've got some right now," Wyatt says. "Also."

Nurse Cara narrows her gaze. "A philosopher-baker," she says.

"We've come about the hopper," K says.

"I guessed as much."

"I believe that Joseph has been in touch on the matter," Wyatt says, sounding twice as old as she is. "Joseph Bell. Special dispensation." Wyatt can get up on her heels sometimes. If you love her you forgive her.

Nurse Cara rifles through files. Taps the computer, wakes up the screen. She chews while she searches, leans forward, scrolls. "Ahhh," she says to herself. She punches some numbers into a phone and walks away. K slices himself a piece of cake while we wait.

Wyatt glares him down.

He shrugs.

"Don't," I say, "start."

Nurse Cara ends her call, returns.

"You'll need a chaperone," she says. I'm thinking Nurse Cara is breaking some rules. For us, maybe. For the hopper?

# TEN

NURSE CARA WAVES US THROUGH. Our shoes squeak. The machines bleep. At the farthest room, Nurse Cara pulls the curtain back. She steps aside and lets us through.

"She isn't talking," Nurse Cara explains, "but she's awake."

The room is dark except for the machines. By the light of the screens I see her—her plaster-casted legs piled high on pillows, her arm like a mummy's, her face swollen into colors I can't read. There are no more sticks or leaves in her hair. On the table by her bed is a jar of wildflowers.

"Do you remember us?" Wyatt asks, quiet.

"We're the ones—" K says.

She doesn't blink.

"Who watched you," I say. "Down at the Muni."

"You're some hopper," Wyatt says. "That was some storm."

And it's nothing, nothing, nothing, and our voices grow softer, softer, softer, and now the silence is the only thing there is, and I wonder what she remembers of us and the forest's dark floor. I wonder if she remembers my hand in her hand, her head in Wyatt's hand, Everest's red shirt sleeves tied around her. We stand for a time at the foot of her bed. Nurse Cara stands closer to her head.

"Wyatt bakes," K says now. "This," he points, "is Wyatt. That's Sophie. I'm K." He takes the cake box from Wyatt and sets it down beside the jar of flowers, and they are Muni flowers, I realize, and the jar is a Mason jar, and so, I think, Joseph's been here.

"It's a cake," Wyatt says. "Just in case."

The girl presses deep into her pillows. She looks like she wants to be anywhere but where she is. I wonder about the pain she's in, the itch of the gauze, her saying nothing, not even looking at the cake.

"We wanted you to know—" I say.

"That we're here," Wyatt finishes.

"That you'll be okay," K says.

She looks from the box to Wyatt, from Wyatt to me, from me to K to Nurse Cara. When she opens her mouth nothing comes out but a moan.

"You must hurt," I say, "—a lot."

"Storm came on so fast," Wyatt says.

"Turning the dawn into the day," K says. "That's what we'd say whenever you'd go hopping."

Pure hopper silence.

"We'd watch," Wyatt says. "Oh, we'd watch."

"It's like you painted the skies," I say. "Really," I say. "I wish you could have seen yourself."

"She's had quite a fall," Nurse Cara says now, covering the hopper's good hand with her own and giving a squeeze. "Healing takes time." The hopper turns her head. She looks away. We're the farthest thing from what she wants and the only people here.

"I know," Wyatt says, but her eyes are full, and when it's time to leave she's the first one out the door.

# ELEVEN

"HOW'D IT GO?" Grandma Aubrey calls in her breathing-hard way, when she hears me in the hallway. It's afternoon.

"Not," I start.

"As planned?" she says. "As hoped for?"

"I guess."

"Which?"

"Both."

I duck into her room and plunk on her bed. I scoot to the center so I won't slide. Used to be that Grandma Aubrey weighed so much that I could sit anywhere on her queen mattress and be just fine. That's not how it is anymore.

"But you saw her," she asks.

"We did."

"How is she?"

"Crushed."

"And—"

"Not talking. Not even a little bit."

"She must be in shock," Grandma Aubrey says, and now Harvey meows, and I gather him up from the floor and head to the window. Watch the cows that I can see from here, the rise and fall of the hills.

"That cat could use a little litter attention," Grandma Aubrey says.

"I will."

"And the mail," she says now. "The mail came."

I release the cat and head down the hall. I lift the mailbox lid, grab the batch, sift through the bills and the junk. I'll write the checks later, and Grandma Aubrey will sign. I'll post them and then go to the bank. Everything here is in her name and mine. Everything now is anticipating later.

*You'll be glad*, Grandma Aubrey says.

I will not.

Now in the clump of the junk of the mail I notice a lavender page. A flyer, courtesy of Gilbertine, Office of the Mayor, folded twice.

**$10,000**

**REWARD**

On the morning of August 22, a teen girl of approximately 13 years of age fell from the sky into the woods near the municipal airport following the failure of her cloud hopper during a storm.

Any verifiable information pertaining to the victim's identity will be rewarded.

**CALL THE TIP LINE: (888) 555-1875**

Out on the road a pickup truck rushes by, leaking Spanish music through the windows.

"Sophie?" Grandma Aubrey asks.

"In a minute." I pick up the phone, head into my room, close the door, call Wyatt.

"You check your mail?" I say when she answers.

"Been helping Joseph scrub the envelope," she says. "What's in the mail?"

"A flyer," I say. "Ten-thousand-dollar reward for info pertaining to the hopper."

The phone goes quiet.

"Ten thousand?"

"Says so right here. On lavender."

I hear Joseph in the background, maybe Sam. I hear the rev of a biplane coming in, wheels screeching on the tarmac. I hear nothing from Wyatt.

"K around?" I ask.

"On errands with Everest," she says.

Joseph calls. She muffles the phone. She comes back.

"Be here tomorrow," she says. "Early. We'll have a meeting. Make a plan."

"If we win the reward we're giving it to the hopper," I say. "That part will be part of the plan."

"Roger that," she says.

One year ago I didn't know anyone named Wyatt.

Now I know her so well, I knew before I even said the words that she would roger them.

*You pick the best people for your life*, Grandma Aubrey always says. *And you stick with them.* I didn't pick, but I would have picked my Grandma Aubrey, and who wouldn't have picked Wyatt and K? The original Sophie Blanchard would have liked them too. She'd have flown across the skies with them. She'd have bought them silk and feathers.

"Sophie?" Grandma Aubrey calls when I hang up.

"Yeah?"

"Everything all right?"

"Coming."

I stand in my room looking out toward the slice of green and rolling hills and the sky that is half blue and part pink and, over there, cloudy. I think of all the ways people can fall out of the sky, the plenty of stories. Half of them I know from the books people left in the Little Free Library outside the house in the valley, and half of them I know from Grandma Aubrey, who said that sometimes balloons knock up against a change of wind, and sometimes they are blown into walls or into wires or into trees, and sometimes the people flying the balloons don't know where they're flying, they're just flying, and I don't know what the hopper's story is, I don't know whether she was being chased or whether she was chasing, whether she lost control or the whole thing was on purpose, whether she was glad we found her or mad we did.

I don't know anything, and no one knows who she is, but we will know who she is—me and Wyatt and K and the vets of the Muni. We'll know first because we know best. We know best because we all know what it is to lose something. What it is to be afraid. We're smart on that.

"Got us some ice cream," I tell Grandma Aubrey now, because I do.

I settle in. I get Harvey fixed up. I pull the lavender page from my pocket, show it to Grandma Aubrey.

Her eyebrows go up in her head.

"Wyatt wants to take the lead," I say.

"Of course she does."

"I'm taking the lead with her."

"Of course you are."

I kiss the space between Harvey's ears. He touches his tongue to his nose then gives his vanilla a taste, and we all three watch the window between slurps.

# TWELVE

IT RAINED LAST NIGHT and into dawn. No flying at Air Time. I cut through a back door wearing an old coat and a pair of jeans ripped short at the hem and the blue rubber boots I found in the cottage on the day Grandma Aubrey and I moved in. The birds scatter when they hear my boots squeak. They sprinkle like black pepper. I walk through the old planes of the hangar, past the Beechcrafts and the Champ and the Tri-Pacer, their wheels melting into the concrete floor, their windshields crazing, by which I mean the windshields are all shattered. These are the crash vehicles that nobody's fixed. This is the land of K. When I live here, because someday I'll live here, I will not live in a plane.

The Skyhawk has a long snout and stiff ears, and there is the smell of crumbs and fruit.

"K?" I call.

He's there, past the cockpit glass. His eyes like twin lights and a sheet from Wyatt's line pulled to his chin, his cloud of hair. He cracks the cockpit door, stands, and climbs down. He's got his zebra-colored sneakers on, the laces loose. His khakis are weathered in the knees. The birds rain down from the rafters and splash around K's feet. It's all those crumbs they're after.

K doesn't know how he looks to me.

K doesn't know how I wonder about the secrets he keeps. About his mom and where she is. About his dad and if he knew him. About the things he doesn't say he wants, but he has to want something, sleeping in a Skyhawk. He has to want something, his namesake being the alphabet, his life a bunch of borrow.

"You see Wyatt?"

He starts walking.

I start walking.

Out the front door, across the tarmac, past the American flag and the REST IN PEACE sign beside the plane that took a nosedive and was left right where it fell. Past the tower across the open, tall-grass fields. There are still lines through the grass from where we ran the day the hopper fell, where the men ran, where the ambulance drove, and we can see where Wyatt has been, the squish of her bootprints over the flattened grass.

We clap our hands in front of our faces to keep the bugs away. We reach the edge where the trees begin. We follow the fresh bootprints in the new mud and swat at the bugs and listen to the caw of the birds, and I wish Wyatt had waited for us, but that's not Wyatt. It's not that she has to be first, it's that she can't stop herself.

"Wyatt?" we call. She doesn't answer.

The songbirds in the tall trees are better than the ravens in the high sky. The old berries look new on old thorns. There are pine needles and the *pop pop pop* of the ground at our feet and the swish of the low branches that we elbow out of our way. Up ahead is the creek. We cross it. Beyond that is the clearing in the woods, like someone cut a hole out of the trees, but the hole is more of a rectangle than a circle, and the trees around the hole, the closest ones to the hole, look like someone took a match to them, like they stand in permanent singe. Wyatt isn't that far now, Wyatt and her light beam, and why she needs one in the daytime I cannot say, except that in some parts of the woods it does get dark, on account of all the shelter of the trees.

But not in this part. Not in the clearing. Call it a skylight, this black hole in the trees.

Wyatt's got the long side of her hair tied up in a one-clump pigtail. She's got a canvas bag hooked to her shoulder, a pair of gloves snug on her hands. She's on her hands and knees, digging, it looks like, with her fingers. The balloon and the burner and the propane pack of the hopper are gone—dragged out by the police, tagged and stashed in an evidence locker, according to what Everest said. The biggest proof of the hopper's fall is what broke when she fell. The snapped limbs of the trees at the edge of the clearing. The scrubbed-off bark of those trees. The skids and the dents and the little craters in the ground.

"Yo," K says.

Wyatt doesn't answer.

"Earth to Wyatt."

"Had a concept," Wyatt says.

"A concept?"

"Actually, factually yes."

"So?"

There's no hurrying Wyatt. K and I crouch to see what her fingers have found.

Earthworms.

Slugs.

Tiny sticks.

A circle of metal.

A knot of rope.

A broken-up board that was already broken, if I'm guessing right, before the hopper fell.

Old things and rust things. Junker things.

Wyatt has it all laid out, collected.

"This isn't it," she says.

"Isn't what?" K asks.

"What I'm looking for."

She duckwalks forward, still crouched. She sweeps her gloved hands across the earth, her flashlight shining where her hands are sweeping. K and I fan out a little. We sweep our hands too. The birds sing and we sweep and that's it.

"What are we looking for?" I ask.

"Anything that tells us anything," Wyatt says.

We clap our hands to scare away the bugs. We keep sweeping. A couple of screws, some chunky wood splinters, the nozzle from a tank, a twist of threads. We collect what we collect, whatever trash the police left here as trash. Wherever Wyatt works she shines her beam of light. Sometimes it's brighter than the sun.

"Hey," K says now. "Check this out."

Wyatt and I uncrouch and hurry to K's side. He stands and opens his hand. It's an origami bird. Faded and flimsy and used to be pink. Like the birds that hang from Grandma Aubrey's ceiling.

Wyatt lifts it with care. She lays it flat on her own palm.

"Light, please," she says, and K goes to get her beam.

She lifts the paper bird by a finger pinch of her gloves, holds it high, shines the light through.

"Look," she says, and we see what she sees.

Words inside the bird.

Two words.

Handwritten.

On the closest log with the mossiest seat we sit. We hardly breathe. Crease by crease, Wyatt opens the origami wings, the neck, the beak until the bird is just a square of paper, faded pink on one side, blue words on the other.

"*Mauricio Flores,*" Wyatt says, reading the words out loud.

# THIRTEEN

BACK AT THE MUNI, Everest has heard the news. *Ten thousand dollars.* He's been to the hardware store and to Gas Guzzler. He was at the post office and the pharmacy. He was even at the Twenty Four, where everybody's missing Wyatt's blues, he says, and the talk is pure lavender flyer.

The tip line.

The news.

That reward.

The social worker who thinks she has an explanation and the police who are stumped and the someone who wants to start a GoFundMe to pay for the hopper's hospital care and the other someones who have ugly things to say about people who might be like the hopper: *They should go back to where they came from. They are dirty. Lock them up.* Everyone has theories: The hopper won't talk because she's afraid.

The hopper won't talk because she can't. The hopper won't talk because English is not her language. The hopper won't talk because no one has asked her the right question. Nurse Cara was on the morning TV they were playing at the diner, Everest says, answering reporters with her ponytail swinging left and right when the answer was no and up and down when it was yes, and mostly it was no because she's no official spokesperson, she's just someone they're harassing when she's in the parking lot and because she's trying to keep what she can keep confidential, except there's a reward out for information, and everyone has questions.

Everest has a bolt in one hand, a screw in the other. He looks past us when he talks, through the parasail windows, like he's seeing Vietnam out there—jungle green and combat, medevac and triage, big birds overhead. I don't know anything about that part of his life except for all the medals. I don't know what he sees until he turns back to us.

"You've been out in the woods," he says. "At the crash site."

I have no idea how he knows. Maybe the mud on our knees, the mud in our fingernails. Wyatt nods.

"Police have been out there already."

"Yeah," K says. "We know."

"Police are thorough."

"Right," Wyatt says.

He raises one of his eyebrows. She raises one of hers. She pulls the origami bird out of her pocket, unfolds its wing. She extends her hand toward Everest, and he digs into his pocket for his glasses.

"Mauricio Flores," he reads, turning the unfolded bird over again. "Anything else?"

"Nothing else," K says.

Everest jiggles the keys in his pocket, heads to the Air Time office, unlocks the door. He sets us up with the computer and the phone books—the new one, a couple of old ones, nobody throws anything away at the Muni. He stands there while we work, then goes away and comes back with Joseph.

"Anything?" they're asking now.

"Nothing yet," Wyatt says.

"Maybe we should ask," K says, "for help. Maybe we should call the police, tell them the name, see if that could help us help the hopper?"

"No," Wyatt says, practically shouts it. "No police."

K stares at her, then looks away, the thing he does when he's counting to ten inside, or sometimes five, counting to keep chill when Wyatt has a moment. "I thought the point," he says, "was to help the hopper. We're coming up with zero here, in case you haven't noticed."

"Not zero," Wyatt says. "We have a name." She takes the origami bird from Everest. She flips it over on her palm, like there'll be something else there when she looks this time, but there's only the one thing: Mauricio Flores.

"K," she says, pacing now, back and forth. "Sorry but—no. I mean—What if Mauricio Flores doesn't want to be found? What if giving up his name means giving up more—means handcuffs and jails and judges and losing whatever else he has going on here, including whatever's going on with the hopper."

"What if it means ICE?" I say. "What if it means cages?"

"I think K has a point," Everest says after a while. "I think there are laws, and—"

"There are laws, and there are *people*," Wyatt says.

She looks from Everest to Joseph to me, back to Everest. We all watch Everest now, and I think about Grandma Aubrey and me a year ago, coming to Gilbertine, a new way to start living when Grandma Aubrey was dying, a fresh page in a new book. I think about the migrants in the fields here who pick the fruit and vegetables we eat and how they just want a chance at something new.

Everest takes the bird from Wyatt's hand. Joseph takes it from Everest's. They turn it over, both of them, like Wyatt did, everybody searching for answers. Not telling the police is wrong, but telling the police seems more wrong, at least until we find out more. Wyatt is sure on it, and I am too, and I can see K coming around and Everest shaking his head and Joseph finally nodding.

"All right," he says, and Everest says "all right" too, and that's how I know for sure, that's how it is decided that we're not giving the name of Mauricio Flores away until we have more answers. We're not trusting anyone but us because we know we can be trusted. Some wrongs are wrong, like I said. Some wrongs are right. This is a missing persons operation. We're missing persons experts: K and Wyatt and me, Everest and Joseph.

"All right," Wyatt says now, exhaling.

I take the bird from Everest's hand. I study it too—its creases, its beak, its smudges. I look at how the hopper formed the words—could be a child's handwriting, as small as it is, as timid, and also crooked. But the hopper is no timid girl. The hopper hopped in a machine that was nothing like a normal hopper. It was a hopper built like a puzzle built from the pieces of separate puzzles. A puzzle hopper. This wasn't some official operation. This was homemade hopping, and that girl hopped, and you'd have to be brave as Sophie Blanchard to get up in the air strapped to that thing.

All power, I think, to the hopper.

All trust among ourselves.

But still: right now we have nothing more than a girl who won't talk and a name we can't place.

# FOURTEEN

IT'S A GOOD-FLY WEEK. We're at Air Time, early.
We're helping Joseph, smoothing the long envelope
of the big balloon out across the tarp, checking the
dawn fliers in—a redheaded man and his kind of
timid wife and their daughter, who is having a birth-
day. We're hauling the inflator fan, completing the
basket and burner check, watching Joseph release
the pibal, looking at each other some of the time,
not asking the questions we're thinking. We hold the
mouth of the envelope open so the inflator fan can
swell the thing with cold air. When it's time, when
the envelope is good and swollen and vertical, Joseph
will put his captain hat on and call the passengers in
and tilt the burner up and blast and blast, and the
thing will lift up from the ground.

It's a beautiful thing, every time.

It hits my heart with a pound.

I think of the girl in the hospital, grounded.

The name in the crease of a bird.

I look at Wyatt. I look at K. I know what they are thinking.

"Going up," Joseph says.

Joseph burns and the balloon lifts into the dawn-burst sky, the white-silver-white, the silence above the noise of the flame. The faces grow smaller smaller smaller in the sky. It's like listening to awe, that burner burning, and it's a good day for a boxed ride, so the balloon will circle back in time. It will cast its shadow onto farms and dogs and roads and streams and steeples, the circle of surrounding hills.

It's hardly eight a.m. Everest and Sam will take it from here, manage the balloon on the back end of the flight. The three of us head to Wyatt's factory. Another bake, and this time we'll have the radio on. We'll pour and stir and taste and clean, and soon we'll go visit the hopper.

# FIFTEEN

THE OWL-EYE GLASSES LADY waves us on, says she'll skip the treat; her clothes are tight.

"Lemon pound cake," Wyatt says. "Blueberry frosting."

"Oh, honey," she says. "Don't tempt me."

We head down the hall to Trauma, hit the square button, wait for the magic double doors. A doctor comes out. A doctor's assistant. Nurse Cara's with a patient. Yam takes off his face mask.

"Lemon pound," Wyatt says.

"Wow," he says.

When Nurse Cara shows up, she takes a bite, leads the way. We head down the hall, and she pulls back the curtain. The hopper sits straighter in the bed. The skin around her eye is a different shade of purple.

"Brought you some blues," Wyatt says.

The hopper turns. When Wyatt does her big

blues reveal, the hopper reaches for the cake with her one good hand, takes a bite while we are watching.

She swallows.

Wyatt smiles.

A victory.

There are a thousand things we want to know. There are all the questions we can't ask her. *Keep it casual*, Wyatt had called out to us, on the bike ride over. Casual. So that's what we are. Just standing here while the hopper's eating.

"I've made some adjustments," Wyatt says, in her best nonchalant, "to an old recipe."

"All berries are fresh, picked straight from the bushes," she continues.

"Blues make everything better," K says.

The hopper eats the whole thing.

She puts the fork down.

She turns to watch the window.

She doesn't turn to us again.

We all just stand there, and the silence is big. The silence is all there is. It is important, Nurse Cara says after a while, to let the hopper rest.

I look at Wyatt who looks at K, and now K looks at me, and I shrug.

One by one by one, we leave, Wyatt leaving last. She keeps one hand in her pocket on that bird in her pocket on that name we did not mention: *Mauricio Flores*.

# SIXTEEN

IT'S A LONG BIKE RIDE HOME.

It's the Schwinn, the double yellow lines, the cows and the farms and the sometimes music of the long, wide farms, the music of the pickers in the middle of the harvest inside the circle of the hills in the boxed air of Gilbertine, and maybe some of the pickers, or some one of the pickers, knows the story of the girl who fell out of the sky or knows the story of Mauricio Flores or knows about the ten-thousand-dollar reward, and even so, won't say a word.

"Well," Grandma Aubrey says when I get home.

"Yeah," I say.

And we just sit, and a breeze blows in, and Harvey meows.

# SEVENTEEN

PLENTY OF WORK AT THE MUNI. Plenty of people going up and down, and sometimes when we're done one of the old pilots will want to know how the hopper is, and we'll stop in the lounge and tell him. K will pop a PayDay out of the vending machine. Wyatt will throw away the microwave trash. I'll clean up the magazines the pilots toss.

"Any news on the hopper?" the pilots will ask. Our secret has become their secret. Their team has become ours. We have ourselves a together goal: find the hopper's story first. Keep her safe. But nothing.

"Anything we can do?" Mikey will ask, or Sam.

"Any missions we can run?"

"Hopper's not talking," I'll say, or Wyatt will say, and the fact is that the hopper's story is fading from the front-page news, and nobody's been handed the reward for information that somebody knows (somebody has to know), and we ourselves have turned up zilch, and it hurts like fire in the bones. K only has one letter for a name and no mother looking for him and nothing but a bunch of hand-me-downs in the Skyhawk where he sleeps, by which I mean that he's never had good answers for himself, so he wants answers for the hopper. Wyatt's baking her blues with her whole blueberry heart and her blueberry fingertips, and the deliciousness of what she bakes has not cracked the hopper mystery. The vets are guys who, years ago, carried best friends out of a war in slings and crawled beneath the spin of helicopter blades and sewed their own patches onto their patched-up coats—but they too have come up hopper empty.

And me? I'm named for Sophie Blanchard—so very famous, so extremely brave—and what have I achieved that's namesake worthy?

Today it's a rain day, and there's no balloon flying. Today it's dark out there and wet, and when I show up anyway, my hair is a mess down my rained-on back, my Schwinn is full of mud out in the rack, the tips of my fingers are numb from holding onto the handlebar too tight. I find Sam and Everest and

Joseph together, a map spread out on the messy lounge table and a bunch of spots circled in red. I lean over to look, but I don't understand. Sam is the one who explains.

"Looking for possible hopper sites," he says.

"Abandoned warehouses, barns, open land," Joseph says. "Anywhere a hopper could hop from."

"Couldn't that be practically anywhere?" I say. "In Gilbertine?" Half the barns are falling down. Half the land is open. Half the trucks that used to ride these roads are parked in places no one seems to own, rusting out to copper tones. And then all those hills in a circle.

"If someone's been hopping from the same exact locale, there could be signs," Everest says. "Landscape wear and tear. Evidence of an inflator fan."

"We're thinking of running some surveillance," Joseph says. "We're narrowing options."

I lean in closer. I see Gilbertine from up above. Sam pops the cap back onto the red-tipped pen and leans back, crossing his arms over his potbelly.

"Three or four dozen sites," he says, "that could be of interest."

"Three or four dozen?" I say.

"It's a starting place," Joseph says. "For now."

"So what's the plan?"

"Working on it."

"Wyatt know?"

"Sure as hell," Sam says. "You think we do any-thing around here without Wyatt?"

"Right," I say. "You know where she is?"

"Back where she always is," Joseph says. "Last time I saw her."

I wait for something else, something more about the plan, the sites, the flyover scheming, but the pilots have forgotten that I'm here. The birds have come inside due to all the outside rain. I hear their flutter. I hear a wrench fall down, the low tones of a radio, and now I head through the Muni, out the parasail door, between the slats of the fence, toward the Hope blueberry farm, and Wyatt.

# EIGHTEEN

SHE'S GOT A COTTON DRESS ON, a pair of lacy tights, her yellow boots. She's got three bowls going at the exact same time and the oven on, a whip in one hand, a spoon in the other, four milky measuring cups by the sink beside her lavender-colored measuring spoons.

She leaves the spoons on the counter when she sees me. She pulls a stool into place and climbs up and pulls back the curtain that hangs in the factory's front window.

"Check this out," she says, pointing.

A bunch of sticks and some string. Looks like a kid's art project. "What?" I say.

"A hummingbird nest. Must have been here a long time and I didn't know it."

She turns it over, so I can see its bottom parts. She turns it right side up, holds it steady on the palm of her hand. She gets lost in a thought I cannot follow.

"Don't you get it?" she says.

I shake my head.

"It was hiding in plain sight," she says.

"This have something to do with the hopper?" I say.

"There's something," Wyatt says, "that we're not seeing."

"That's obvious," I say. "Enough."

Her jacket hangs from the doorknob. She reaches into its left pocket. She takes out the paper bird again, unfolds its creases, reads the words with her best Spanish accent.

*Mauricio Flores.*

She looks up at me. Shakes her head. "Who is he?"

I shrug. I don't know. We've been through it a thousand times before—K and Wyatt and me, Grandma Aubrey, Joseph and Everest and Sam and all the other pilots. We've been over this and on the computer and into the phone books, and still she's asking like I might know the answer. Or like maybe she does.

"Brother, father, uncle, friend. It's one of those," Wyatt says, "and she can't tell us."

"I know."

"Why can't she?"

"It's her secret."

"Why is it her secret?"

"I don't know," I say. "We all have secrets."

She gives me a look.

"What do you mean by that, precisely."

"Forget it, Wyatt."

"No. Seriously. What do you mean?"

"There's something," I say, "that you're not saying. Some reason this is so big for you. I mean, it's big for us too, don't get me wrong. But you, Wyatt—you—"

"Forget it," she says, turning the paper bird over and over in her hands.

"Wyatt?"

"Come on, Wyatt."

"Just look at me, Wyatt."

"You know what they're doing out there? In the Muni?" I say.

"Yes."

"You think that could help solve the riddle?"

"Anything is possible. But it's a long shot. Dozens of sites. Dozens of possibilities."

She folds the origami wings and slips the bird back

in her pocket, stops talking. She pours her batter into tins, slides the tins into the oven. "A simple blueberry crumble," she says, back in her baking voice. "Mixed three ways." Now she clicks the timer on, opens the factory door, and starts walking.

That's it.

That's all.

I follow.

"Wyatt?"

"Yeah."

"Are you mad?"

"No."

"I don't know who Mauricio Flores is."

"I know," she says. "Me, either."

"I don't know why the hopper won't talk or why no one has come to claim her."

"I know."

"Don't be mad."

"I'm not."

"Maybe we should think again about telling the cops," I say, hating the words as soon as I say them. "About what we know."

"No," she says. And that's it. Of course that's it. I shouldn't have even said it.

We don't head to the bushes, we don't head to the Muni, we go straight to the house of Joseph Bell, where Wyatt lives and where someday I'll live too. That's what everybody says. *There's room for you here. When you're ready.* How can I ever be ready? Being ready means being ready to see Grandma Aubrey go. No. Nope. Not. I will never be ready.

*You're the bravest girl I know,* Grandma Aubrey will say.

And I want to say that I am not as brave as she thinks I am, as she needs me to be, as the original Sophie Blanchard. I could not have done what the first Sophie did, at the end, when her whole world went up in flames.

Can't even think about.

Won't.

Sometimes I wonder what it is that K can't think about, won't, what Wyatt can't think about, won't, what would happen if we all confessed to sometimes not being brave.

The Bell house isn't far. It's just a short weedy path to the red door and blue shutters. Wyatt turns the knob, and she's in and down the center hall and into her room. There's a square window on every side but one. A black feather wreath hangs from a bow on the knob and above the wreath, from a hook, hangs a 'Nam jacket, oversized and empty. On a big plaid chair there's a wooden doll, and beside the doll is a velvet pillow, and on the wall are dozens of spoons, each one nailed into place. There's an arrow yanked from a weather vane. There's a laminated map of the world.

Someday there'll be a second bed.

Glass jars on the windowsills, paperbacks on the floor, dictionaries and newspapers, an upside-down helmet painted Army green, and inside the helmet's empty place, where a head might be, is the start of a blueberry bush. Where there is no rug there is a wide-planked floor, and in the planks are scratches, long and thin, like Wyatt took a hoe to them. Over against the far wall is a shoebox without a lid, and inside the box is a blue baby's hat, a boy's baby blue, and a flower scarf and a pair of thin white gloves.

Wyatt sees me eyeing that, like I've eyed it in the past, and I will not, because I don't, ask her about it.

She grabs a wad of newspaper from the newspaper pile and lays the right one down across the bed. She flips through and through until she finds the page she wants, the very last page of the *Gilbertine Gazette*. It's a WE'RE RELOCATING ad. The *we're relocating* is a Doc Martens outlet store.

"Not following," I say.

"Don't you see?" she says.

"You're buying boots?" I say.

"I don't need boots," she says.

"You're—" I start to ask, and then I stop.

"Patent pinks," I say.

"Precisely," she says.

"Right?"

"You're thinking—"

"That maybe she bought her Docs in that outlet store. Maybe there are records. Credit card records. With her name and number. Maybe we can find out through the Docs where she lives, and if we find out where she lives the planes won't have to fly surveillance."

"I don't think the pilots are minding the thought of some surveillance."

"Dozens of sites, like you said. Dozens could take, like, forever."

"So we go with the Doc Martens."

"They're *pink* Doc Martens."

"I know."

"And *patent leather*."

"Right."

"How many people do you know who would buy a pair of Docs like that?"

"Docs could have been a gift," I say.

"True."

"She could have paid with cash. Probably paid with cash if she paid at all. Do you even have a credit card?"

Wyatt shakes her head.

"Do I?" I shake my head. "No. Frankly, I do not."

"That too."

"Plus, whoever bought them, however they bought them—they could have been bought anywhere."

"If there's a chance of a chance," Wyatt says, "we should chase it."

I take another look at the ad. I read the address. I try to think if that's any road I've ever seen, if I can calculate the distance. Wyatt watches my face to read my thoughts. I turn to get some thinking privacy.

"She could have gotten them secondhand," I say.

"It's about ten miles," Wyatt says. "Everest can drive us."

"Today?"

"I'm just waiting on the cakes. Figure they couldn't hurt with our negotiations."

"You're planning on bribing the people who work at Doc Martens?"

"I'm planning on bringing them blues. It's a winning strategy. Obviously."

"Then what?"

"See what they say. Learn what we learn. Every fact we can find can help us."

"Help *her*, you mean," I say.

Wyatt bites her lip.

She looks away.

She touches the scar on her arm.

The scar is the secret she won't tell.

# NINETEEN

WE RIDE FOUR ACROSS in Everest's truck. It's tight, but we make the squeeze, the cakes stacked tall in three boxes on Wyatt's lap. Everest's pickup's got a low bumper and a dent in one door. He's got jazz on the radio. The cornstalks in the cornfields on the side of the roads are catching the sun, and there are coins of ponds and silver silos, steam rising off the heaps of horse poop, the hoed lines of the farms, the broken things collecting copper rust, the pickers picking, the hilly ridge. Sometimes, on the road there's some lavender tumbleweed. Ten-thousand-dollar rewards left to the wind.

Black Harleys streak by.

Everest is telling sky stories as if stories are cushions you could put your tired head down on.

"The earth is on a tilt," he's saying, a lesson in sky. "Amazing what you can see from up above."

He says that at 2,000 feet you get yourself clear of any interference—kites and towers and things. He says that at 5,000 feet you feel the air thin. At 10,000 feet your lungs get themselves a marathon ache, and your lips are blue, and all you want to do is sleep.

"Fifteen thousand feet and you can see the planet spin," Everest says. "You can see the shine and heat. The geography of time."

"Geography of time?" K says.

"Can't you go any faster?" Wyatt says.

Everest *umphs* the accelerator. He's quiet, and then he starts talking again.

The houses run closer together, and they're real houses. The gas stations are twinned with mini-marts. There's no more horse and buggy and no girl on roller skates, and now here's the outlet store in a veritable outlet haven. One discount dealer beside the other. Lots of cars and Everest's truck. Lots of stores, and in every store there is a percentage sign. Twenty percent off. Thirty percent off. Fifty. At the Doc Martens outlet it is the buyers' lucky day. Take another ten percent off the thirty percent off, or buy two for the price of one and a half.

We open the door.

The bell rings.

I get stuck for a minute on all the Doc Martens boots topping off the boxes that run up and down the outlet's rows. Doc Martens that look like graffiti walls. Doc Martens that look like paint blots. Doc Martens in patent red and pink and blue and ones that look like the Renaissance paintings Grandma Aubrey and I studied this spring, in our homeschool art class. Doc Martens green as a parrot and white as a goose and sly as a fox and all that yellow stitching around each sole was hand sewing-machined on, according to the posters that show the step by step of the Docs' manufacture. Which takes place in England, by which I mean a factory in—

"Sophie," Wyatt whispers. "Pay attention."

Pay attention to her, she means. Pay attention to how, right now, Wyatt has her eye on a clerk with two arm sleeves of tattoos. A pretty teenager with a hoop in her nose, who is ringing up an old-lady customer, bagging up the lady's boots, handing over a receipt, waving goodbye, and now there's nobody else in the store, and it's our turn.

Wyatt's turn.

"Hello," the clerk says. "You here for some boots?"

"Here to talk about boots," Wyatt says. "But first: Do you happen to fancy blueberries?"

Wyatt extends the boxes in her hands.

The clerk gets a whiff of the crumble.

Looks confused.

"I'm the baker for the Twenty Four, down the road, about ten miles," Wyatt starts. "This is a crumble, mixed three ways. Fresh out of the oven. Thought you might like some."

"You're the Twenty Four baker?" the clerk says. Scratches her head. "Yes," she says. "You are. I've seen you there. I've had your pie. Your pies are just outrageous."

Wyatt beams, head to toe.

"It's your lucky day then," K says. "What we have here is bona fide crumble." Everest stands close to the door, with his hands crossed over his chest. Not looking like he wants to leave, not looking, either, like he'll interfere. This is Wyatt's operation. He is, to use K's words, merely facilitating. He has a look on his face.

"We have a question," Wyatt says now, placing the boxes on the counter beside the register.

"Yes?"

A new customer opens the door, steps past Everest, begins her journey up and down the rows of boots.

"We notice you sell pink patent leather Docs," Wyatt says.

"We do," the clerk says. "What size are you?"

The clerk has slipped her finger under the lid of a Wyatt crumble box. She's popped the lid. She's taking in the aroma. She breathes deep. Breathes deep again. Wyatt finds the spoon she always carries in her pocket. Dangles it across the counter.

"Definitely my lucky day," the clerk says. "I will have to acquiesce. To all hell with my diet."

"Acquiesce is a good word," K tells her.

"I'm a writer," the clerk says. "This is just my day job."

Wyatt smiles. This is going really, *really* well. This is going really better than really well. The clerk likes blues. The clerk's a fan of Wyatt's. The other customer is just strolling around, and there's time, and Wyatt is so good at asking questions.

"Not looking to buy myself," she says. "Though someday, when I get enough in savings, I'm going to get myself a pair for sure. Maybe the graffiti. Maybe the zebra stripes. Right now in this minute I'm just looking for information on behalf of a friend. Weird question, I know, but: You have any recollection of the customers who have gone in for the pinks?"

"Recent?"

"Could be.

"Well," the clerk says.

"I'm thinking of one customer in particular. A girl, maybe twelve, maybe thirteen-fourteen. Short curly hair? Big brown eyes? Darker skin than mine?"

"You're asking if someone like that came in here to buy the pinks?" the clerk says, her mouth half full of crumble.

Wyatt nods.

"Oh man," the clerk scratches her ear, pulls gently at her nose. "You would be testing my memory, wouldn't you?"

"We have time," Wyatt says. "We can wait. Here," she points to the crumble. "Have another spoonful."

The clerk chews and swallows, chews and swallows. She looks at Wyatt. She is trying to decide, I decide, what she should confide to Wyatt. How many of her own questions she should ask. How much she should just tell Wyatt, because.

Are there retail laws like there are hospital laws?

Is it wrong to tell a stranger about a customer?

Does the clerk suspect what we're looking for here? Is she hoping for her own ten-thousand reward?

The clerk shrugs. "I think," she says, "that I do remember a client like that. I remember because she was so sure about the pink, nothing but pink, and the pink had to shine. And I remember because of her father. And I remember because it wasn't that long ago. Maybe eight weeks. Maybe ten."

"What?" Wyatt asks, "about her father?"

"The way he spoke to her," the clerk says. "And not just the Spanish."

"What else?" Everest asks.

"Yeah," the clerk says, "kind of hard not to remember. Handsome dude. Big arms. Strong hands."

"Nice guy?" Wyatt asks.

"Seemed to be."

"Young?"

"Not very old. She wanted pink boots. He helped her buy them."

"*You,*" Everest says, "are being helpful."

The clerk seems to like the sound of that. The clerk, I decide, likes to be helpful.

"Did they buy with a check?" Wyatt asks, her face dark, her mouth tense. "With a credit card?"

"No," the clerk says, and she's on a roll now. She is not going to stop. "Nothing like that." K watches. Wyatt bites her bottom lip. "It was cash. Definitely cash. A bunch of crumpled dollar bills. Kind of dirty. Plenty of ones, a couple of fives. Not something I'd forget, now that I remember."

Wyatt exhales.

Her whole body deflates like one of her Dutch pancake blues once you put a fork on it.

"Cash," Wyatt says.

"Yeah," the clerk says.

"You're sure?"

"I mean, yeah. I'm sure. The boots were on discount, you know. Like everything."

"So there's no—" I say.

"No record," the clerk says. "If that's what you want." She pushes the crumble away. Puts the spoon down. "I shouldn't have even told you—"

"You did great," Everest says.

"Terrific," K says.

"I'm so glad you were here," Wyatt recovers, "and that you like crumble."

"*Like* crumble?" the clerk says. "You kidding? I've got a lot of love for your baked creations. You coming here was like a movie star walked in. You coming with this—" She points to the boxes.

"You take the rest home," Wyatt says.

"All three?" the clerk's amazement is pure amazement. It is astonishment.

"Yes," Wyatt says, taking her spoon back, wiping it off on the hem of her shirt.

"We're moving," the clerk says. "The store. You know? We're moving fifteen miles down the road. If you ever want a pair of Docs—"

"Then I'll be your customer," Wyatt says.

"I'm good with the discounts," the clerk says.

"Right," Wyatt says.

"And I sell on credit. And, like I said, I do take cash."

"Will remember that," Wyatt says. As if she could forget. Forget that she was right—that the girl was there. Forget that she was wrong—thinking any of this could help us. The girl was here, and there was a man with her. They spoke Spanish.

*Mauricio Flores.*

Big arms.

Strong hands.
Has to be.
Everest leaves first and then K, then me.
The last of us is Wyatt.

# TWENTY

WE STOP ON THE WAY HOME for Everest errands. We stop at a roadside stand for rhubarb and strawberries. We stop to get some milk and lemon and creamer, some chocolate for K, some grease and screws at the hardware store—everything on Everest. We don't talk too much about the clerk in the store or the story she told about the hopper. Has to be the hopper. Who speaks Spanish. Who paid with cash. Ones and fives and dirty bills. Aren't we sure? Aren't we sure he was her father?

"Be careful," Everest said, when we were leaving. "False assumptions are bad assumptions. We know only what we know."

What do we know?

All of us four across, now, riding in silence.

Up ahead, through Everest's windshield and high in the sky is the Air Time floater. The white-silver-white of the envelope. The razor flame of the burn. The wicker bottom of the basket catching the rays of the sun. Joseph's up, and he's all alone. Joseph's up there, searching.

And now it rises.

And it goes higher.

We all have our eyes on it.

Everest takes a turn, and we slide. Wyatt into me, me into K, and something's changing, something's already changed.

# TWENTY-ONE

"SOPHIE?" Grandma Aubrey calls.

"Here."

"Honey?"

The screen door closes behind me. I head down the hall, poke my head into her room. The breeze through the window has got the dangling things flying.

The dark is coming down on the day. She looks whiter than vanilla. Whiter than her pillow. Harvey is anxious, he's pacing.

"Grandma Aubrey?"

She breathes out, and it makes a hard sound. She breathes in and opens her eyes. I fix the stack of pillows behind her. Tip her forward. Rub her back. She breathes a little easier, but it's still not good, and I don't like it.

"Mauricio Flores," she says. "Your hopper. Any luck. With the . . . Doc Martens?"

I wait for her to catch her breath before I answer.

"She was there," I say. "At the shop. Definitely. She was there with her father."

*No assumptions*, Everest said. But assumptions tell the story quicker.

"And?"

"Nothing. They paid with cash."

"Oh, honey."

"Yeah."

"You'll find—"

"Wyatt's taking it worse than the rest of us."

"Look," Grandma Aubrey continues, and now I see, across her bed, the spread of the newspaper I'd brought in earlier. Front-page pictures of families at the border. Headline: SEEKING ASYLUM.

More pictures:

Babies behind fences.

Mothers behind walls.

A boy younger than me whose father is gone.

Grandma Aubrey starts coughing, can't stop. Her white face turns red. I lay the paper on the floor and sit close beside her. I hand her the glass of water I'd left for her at dawn, when the sun was still bright and when Mauricio Flores was a different kind of hope we had. A man we could find before others find him. A man to get a word to about his daughter.

*Go see her.*

*Go talk to her.*

*She won't talk to any of us.*

Grandma Aubrey won't stop coughing.

"We should call the doctor," I say.

"Dr. Cooley?" she asks.

"Dr. Cooley's five hundred and four miles south," I say.

"And a little east," she says, trying to make a laugh out of her cough, but this isn't funny, nothing is funny. I left the house in hope of hopper news. I've come home to bad news about my grandma.

"I'll call Emergency?"

"What's the emergency?"

"You, Grandma Aubrey. You're the emergency." I hear my voice tick up, too loud. I try to steady it. *Be good.*

"Nothing that is not to be expected," she says, but it takes her way too long to say it, and my thoughts are worries, and my worries are like the black storm in the sky that came upon the hopper and threw her to the ground.

"I am going," I say, "to call."

"This not an emergency," she says. "This is me and how I'm breathing. Best thing for us both is a story."

"No, Grandma." I roll my eyes. "No."

"It's been. A long. Day. A hard day. We both could use a story."

I don't feel like a story. I don't feel like pretending that nothing's going on, like I don't need help, like I'm big enough, even though I'm tall.

"We have any more of that . . . factory jam?" she asks.

"I'm calling," I say.

"I'm in charge," she says. "This too shall pass."

She steadies herself and breathes in a little deeper. She breathes until she almost sounds like she's normal again. She's making a point, and I take her point—we're past emergency. We're just the two of us—the grandmother is better than any mom would ever be; the granddaughter named for the greatest aeronaut the world has ever seen. Two sky fliers, except neither one has left the ground.

"I'll take some ice cream," Grandma Aubrey says, after a while. "Some toast. That story."

She is so tired. Her eyes are nearly closed.

I stand from the bed, head to the kitchen, call over my shoulder about flavors. Think about the hopper, the dollar bills, the stories in the paper. Soon Wyatt and K will go back to school, and I'll stay here, homeschooling. Summer will be over for real, and we won't know more about the hopper.

"How about . . . my third-favorite story," Grandma Aubrey calls, from around the corner.

She wins. She's won.

I scoop the ice cream. I make the toast. I set Grandma Aubrey up with her eat-in-her-bed tray and then cross the room to the newspaper stacks where the third-favorite story lives, the one we call "The Orbiter." The one where everyone you're rooting for wins, even when winning doesn't seem like winning can ever happen.

Best kind of story there is.

"Fine," I say.

"Oh good," she says.

She does her best to smile.

# TWENTY-TWO

I START RIGHT AT THE START, March 1, 1999, with Bertrand Piccard and Brian Jones launching their Breitling Orbiter 3 from Château-d'Oex, by which I mean (we both know I mean) a town in Switzerland. I get the big balloon flying. Southwest over the Mediterranean. Swerving over Mauritania. Now toward Asia and the Pacific Ocean and Central America. The big balloon, the around-the-world floater, is flying. Again. For Grandma Aubrey's sake.

"You see the Orbiter 3, Grandma Aubrey?"

I mean in her mind's eye.

"Oh. I do."

"Isn't she something?"

"She's a wonder, Sophie B. Thank you."

I have the old newspapers spread out where the new newspapers were. The old news tells this story like it's happening right now, today. These are the pages that Grandma Aubrey saved so she would never forget the tale. They're yellow now. They're fading. They smell like old newspaper. They're spread out like a yellow fan beside me on her bed. They're her medicine, that's what they are. They're her medicine, and I'm her doctor, and the treatment plan is a story.

Grandma Aubrey is watching the Orbiter 3 fly with both of her eyes closed.

She's drawing in her breath, letting it out slow.

"Go on."

"The silver balloon is a hundred and eighty feet tall," I read from the newspaper stack. "It's hot air and gas, with a top-floor helium compartment and propane stored up in tanks. It's the best balloon there is for the best balloon adventure there's ever been. A race against time. A race against history. A race to circumnavigate the world in a balloon."

"Isn't it marvelous?" Grandma Aubrey says.

"Mmmm hmmm," I say, and then I think how I can't forget to give K that word: circumnavigate. He'll like it. Lots. If your namesake is the alphabet, you have to make the most of that. I'll give the word to K.

I read the best parts of the best parts aloud. The parts about the meteorologists helping the balloon pilots find the fastest winds. The parts about the solar panels. The parts about the pilots wrangling the currents to stay out of air they're not allowed in and the balloon going as high as 38,507 feet, which is so much higher than Everest ever talks about. I read about how the air inside the diving bell started losing $CO_2$ and how thick teeth of icicles formed on the balloon and how the pilots sawed the icicles off and dropped them to the desert down below. I read through the days of the Orbiter's flight. Sixteen days. Seventeen days. Eighteen. I read through the weather they faced. I read about how the propane fuel on the Orbiter ran low and the balloon kept flying.

"They're going to . . . make it," Grandma Aubrey says.

Just a whisper.

Just some raspy words.

Just her talking to me, an allegory.

Another word for K. *Here*, I'll say to him next time. *Another K-sized word.*

I get up to dampen a towel for Grandma Aubrey. I press it to her forehead. I get up and make her apricot tea. She takes a tiny sip. I fix her pillows, and she leans back, and it's all dark outside by now. There are a couple of lightning bugs lighting up the room. Harvey takes a swat at one. The lightning bug flies on.

Grandma Aubrey asks for more of the story.

"They're headed for the pyramids of Egypt," I say, settling back in and reading from the newsprint. "The winds are getting testy."

"So are the pilots."

"Course they are."

The Orbiter flies. It flies. I read about it flying. I read about how it takes the sky and soars. I read until the Orbiter makes it all around the world. Until it wins the race against time. Crashing down just beyond the Great Pyramids, but coming down safe, just the same. Back on the ground, nobody gone missing.

"They did it," I say, kissing Grandma Aubrey on the cheek.

"Yes," she says. "They did."

She sighs.

She almost dreams.

"Fly," she whispers. "Fly on."

I stack the newspapers up, one by one. I return them to the wall, quiet as I can. I snap on a lamp and find another book, the book called *Earth*, which is one of Grandma Aubrey's favorites.

I snuggle back in beside her. She opens her eyes. I turn the pages so that she can see the pictures of our planet from far up above.

"Oh," she says.

*Live*, the doctor said.

But did he know it would get like this?

Did he know that living's not that easy?

I turn the pages. I say Grandma Aubrey words. The words that she has taught me. Homeschooled, life-schooled, beauty-schooled, live-schooled. It's all the same to Grandma Aubrey. It's all of everything to her. Find the beauty.

"Look," I whisper, and she glances down, but only barely. I turn the pages slowly. I read the words that are there. I say the words that aren't there. I remember when she sang to me. I try to sing to her.

*The calligraphy of streams.*

*The phosphorescent moss.*

*The rugged craters.*

*The blue blur of Eleuthera.*

*The crackled glass of Glacier Park.*

*Hot springs.*

*Great barrier reefs.*

*Fumaroles and karsts.*

The earth from above.

"So much," she says, her voice far away. "Look at all that beauty."

I close the book. I stroke her hair. I watch her face—the dreams beneath her eyelids. Grandma Aubrey does not have long. If I'm not careful now, I could lose her.

# PART TWO

# TWENTY-THREE

IT'D BEEN A HARD NIGHT of sleeping for Grandma Aubrey. It'd been another long day and then another long day, and now everything is different.

Summer is gone. Wyatt and K are back at Gilbertine High. I'm here doing what I can—bringing the news in off the porch, and sometimes I'm beside Grandma Aubrey reading the paper. History, science, current events, literature—it's all in there, even the weather. A whole school day's full of learning beside Grandma Aubrey, and MS is the meanest mean, MS is noisy, and it's selfish, and it's our life now, more than ever.

I can't leave because she cannot leave me.

They've kept the hopper in the hospital. Her bones are still healing, but her stitches are out, and every now and then, they'll flash the reward ad again on the news. And some feature writer will tell the story of looking for the story, and how sometime soon, when she can walk again, maybe Social Services will be finding her a home. She's a ward of the hospital till then—that's what the writers write—and Wyatt and K are most-of-the-time visitors—that is what they tell me.

Sometimes, on either side of school, K will call and ask me to come over. "We need you," he'll say, and I'll think of him in the Skyhawk doing his homework while Wyatt finishes a bake. I'll think of him out in the morning dew scrubbing the big balloon, helping to get the thing up in the sky. Wyatt and K and the Muni pilots were plenty of plenty before I came along. Then I came along, and K is the one who misses me out loud.

"Grandma Aubrey needs me," I'll tell K when he calls. He'll wait like I can change my mind. Then Grandma Aubrey will start coughing but not on purpose, and I won't want K to hang up so I'll ask questions.

"How was school?"

"What'd you learn?"

"Who's the best at gym?"

"Any homework?"

"Any news on the hopper?"

"Zero, zilch on the hopper," he'll say. "Except she still loves Wyatt's blues. Come with us."

"My grandma's bad."

"How about the tomorrow after tomorrow?"

"I guess I'll see tomorrow."

Nothing, and then: "Wyatt says hi. Wyatt says she wishes you would come."

"Tell her hi back."

"Tell your grandma hi. Tell her to get better. Tell her amelioration is the goal."

"Nice one, K. Nice word."

"Yeah."

"You want another word?"

"Sure."

"*Fumaroles.*"

"Sweet."

"Means that place in the volcano where all the bad stuff escapes."

"Even sweeter."

I wait for him to give me a word. He waits for me to say something.

"Call me again," I say now. "Call me tomorrow?"

"I will."

Then neither of us do anything until he hangs up or I do.

When Grandma Aubrey is awake, I read her stories. When she's asleep, I put the Muni in my head—the tunnel of planes and the pilots and the big aerial map and all the circles in red and all the smells of the blues. And K. And Wyatt. Then I'll think about the hopper and the name she pressed into a paper bird and the nothing she will say and all the things that might explain why she won't say it. If you're on the wrong side of things, they take your mothers away. If you don't have proper papers, they take your fathers. If you show up at a hospital somebody could sweep you away like a crumb by a broom. Send you back to the country where you aren't safe.

The facts have weight.

MS has weight too. It's sly, it can't be trusted. It's there, and then it's there too much, and then it's almost everything, and right now it's everything, or it feels like it is, and I can't leave Grandma Aubrey.

So I help her when I can. And I watch her so she won't leave me. And I look for more facts in the in-between times, as if I think facts could actually save me.

Words from the Mayo Clinic website:

144

Multiple sclerosis (MS) is a potentially disabling disease of the brain and spinal cord (central nervous system).

In MS, the immune system attacks the protective sheath (myelin) that covers nerve fibers and causes communication problems between your brain and the rest of your body. Eventually, the disease can cause permanent damage or deterioration of the nerves.

MS doesn't play one bit of nice. Sometimes it's bad, and sometimes it disappears, and then, when it comes back again, it can run fast and furious forward. Also from the Mayo Clinic—words Grandma Aubrey's doctor gave to her and she gave to me so that I would understand the facts, so that I would have them, so that any question I didn't even think to have would get itself answered:

Some people with MS experience a gradual onset and steady progression of signs and symptoms without any relapses. This is known as primary-progressive MS.

You can expect some or all or a bad combination of: muscle spasms, leg paralysis, problems with the bladder or the bowel, memory slips and a hard-knock sadness and up-and-down mood swings. You can expect to be weak in the arms. Sometimes in the legs. Sometimes in the ventilatory muscles, which is why Grandma Aubrey has such a hard time catching air, which is the stupidest thing, because who loves air as much as Grandma Aubrey?

She rattled awake last night, and it scared me.

She stopped breathing this morning when I brought her her applesauce, but only for a fraction of a minute.

She asked for her bedpan, and she hates to ask for that.

She asked for me to sit and read to her.

She asked for me to sit in quiet.

She asked for the bedpan again.

Love takes the embarrassing out of the embarrassing. Maybe K has a word for that.

"Hon," Grandma Aubrey says now, climbing up out of her dreams.

"Yeah?"

"I could use . . . some more Muni tales. Why don't you—"

"We've got plenty of tales," I say. "Plenty of adventures."

"We need some new ones," Grandma Aubrey says.

"I'm good," I say, "with you," and it isn't long before she falls asleep again. I feel the chill blowing through the window we're not closing, and now, after a long time of lots of quiet in between us, the plug-it-in-the-wall phone rings.

Four thirty in the afternoon.

"Sophie?" Wyatt says.

"Hey."

"You should get out."

"Don't think I can."

"She'd like to see you."

"She tell you that?"

"Come on, Sophie. Your grandmother wouldn't mind."

"Anything could happen at any time," I say. "I'm here in case it does."

"Okay," Wyatt says.

"Miss you," I say.

"Yeah," she says, and hangs up.

There are dreams beneath Grandma Aubrey's eyelids. I can see them flutter.

# TWENTY-FOUR

A WEEK.

Ten days.

I Schwinn to the corner store to get what we need. I clean, and I watch, and I sit, and I take care of Harvey, and I read to Grandma Aubrey—the news we can stand, the books we once read, the stories we have memorized. Every day after school Wyatt or K calls, or both of them right after the other. They tell me news, or they tell me there's no news. On Saturdays Wyatt works the diner. On Sundays K and Wyatt both help Joseph with Air Time. The most popular day of the week in autumn for a big floater fly.

September through to October.

October now.

Grandma and Harvey and me and the cows out back and the fields that need less picking and the cars that whoosh by in the street. The window we keep open stays open so that we can see when the big floater floats by. Up in the sky it flies. Bobbing and climbing, white-silver-white.

"Breathtaking," Grandma Aubrey says. And then she's dreaming.

Now the phone rings and it's Wyatt.

"Sophie," she says, her voice up close and near and urgent. "We've got some news over here that you should see."

"News?"

"That's right."

"Hopper news?"

"That's what we think."

"A breakthrough situation?"

"Can't say for sure, but—can't you Schwinn in? Can't you? Just for the afternoon?"

"I don't—I can't . . ."

It goes quiet on the other end. I try to picture Wyatt, calling me, maybe from the rolltop desk or maybe from the house or maybe from the factory, K standing there beside her with the muscles he doesn't even realize that he has.

"Sophie?" Grandma Aubrey calls now, from the other room.

"I'm here," I call back.

"Sophie, if those're your friends on the phone, you better—"

She doesn't get the whole sentence out. She starts coughing.

"Hold on," I say, and put the phone down. Hurry to the bedroom. Rub my grandma's back.

She gets her easy breathing going.

She waves her hand—toward the phone. I get back to Wyatt, who's still there, on the other end, waiting and listening.

"She okay?" she asks.

"I've gotta go," I say. "Miss you guys," I say. "Say hello to the hopper for me."

# TWENTY-FIVE

TWO DAYS LATER, NOON, I'm sitting on Grandma Aubrey's bed, a book laid out, that book called *Earth*, when I hear commotion coming. The rumble of a truck. The rumble of a Harley. Another Harley.

The noise comes in loud through the open window. It flaps the curtains, wakes up Harvey, who had fallen asleep on my toes on the bed. He's been licking the sugar off his whiskers while he sleeps and now opens one eye, and I scooch to pick him up, swoop him to my chest, hoist him up to one shoulder, and go find out what the rumble is.

"What is it?" Grandma Aubrey asks, still half asleep.

"Finding out," I say.

Harvey's tail is a furry pendulum.

His heartbeat thuds my shoulder.

The only thing I see outside is the dust of the rumble that's gone by.

I head to the kitchen.

Stare through the window.

Turn Harvey around so that he can see it too, because maybe my eyes are deceiving.

"Sophie?" Grandma Aubrey calls.

"Yes?"

"That your friends?"

"Seems it could be."

"Give me a minute, hon."

"Give you a minute?"

"Friends are here. We have to get proper."

"Give *me* a minute. I'll help you."

There's a show going on. Right outside the cottage window. There's Wyatt and K and Joseph and Everest and Sam and a truckload of stuff that they're unloading. I watch, mesmerized. Wyatt flapping a purple-plaid down on the green grassy yard. K putting stones on every corner. Everest carrying a basket of plates and spoons and forks and knives to the sheet, and now here comes Joseph with a big silver tin, and Wyatt follows with Tupperware and K with soda bottles and Sam with a funny foldout chair, and now Sam's back with a red blanket and some blue cushions, bending over his belly to get his operation done.

The truck and the Harleys are parked off to the side. The green hills of Gilbertine lie beyond—the cows on the far side of the neighbor's fence. The big tulip trees casting their shade. The clouds in the sky puffing.

I lean across the sink.

I open the window.

"Hey," I call.

"It's a blues holiday," Wyatt says. "On account of your Grandma Aubrey."

"We figured it's Grandma Aubrey Day," K says.

"You gave her a *day*?"

"We figured," Wyatt says, "why not? If you can't come to us—"

"We'll come to you," K finishes, and part of me thinks this idea started there, with K, who might not have the full name of the mother who lost him, who'd rather sleep in a broken cockpit than a bed. K is full of incompletes, which is how he sees so perfectly what's incomplete in others.

Like Wyatt.

Like me.

"Sophie?" I hear Grandma Aubrey calling from her room. "Could use a little help."

"Coming," I say, but I stand watching a little longer. I stand taking the waft of the smell in, the rising fog as they set the dishes out, take the foils off, the lids. Pearl onions and rosemary. Strawberries melted with sugar. Lemon in butter. Roasted chicken. Blues.

"Sophie?" Grandma Aubrey calls.

"It's a party," I tell her.

A jump in my chest where my heart is.

# TWENTY-SIX

HER BEST WHITE OXFORD. Her best sky blue elastic-waist pants. Her best tan orthopedic shoes. Her cane out of the corner and my wet hands patting down her hair. A little lipstick, red, her only lipstick color. A nubby sweater. A Snoopy scarf. She's breathing hard. She's happy.

I call through the kitchen window that it's time. Everest and Joseph hear me, look up, come around to the front and up the porch and down the hall.

I've got a sweater on by now. I've put my hair up in a knot.

"At your service," Joseph says, his turnip nose and ears a little blushy from the weather.

"My handsome chaperones," Grandma Aubrey says, and she lets them help her, slowly they help her down the hall, through the door, across the porch, and around to the yard, where the party is. Three old people with more or less white hair. Two tall. One short. Hard breathing.

Harvey follows.

I follow.

I run back inside to get a second scarf.

Sam is waiting by the foldout chair. He bows, folds the blanket back, puffs the pillows, and the three vets settle Grandma Aubrey in. They fold her and bend her and pull the blanket to her chin. I tie the second scarf around her neck. She coughs. She smiles.

"What a nice . . . surprise," she says.

"It's your day," K says to her. Looking at me. I feel a blush rise up in my cheeks.

"Now is it?"

"Why shouldn't it be?" Wyatt says. She's wearing only one hoop in her ear. She has shadows on her face. Her fingertips are blue. Her tights cling to her skinny legs, her coat is something borrowed, her dark dress hangs like a curtain waiting on the breeze.

K is looking his best—his Sinatra hat on and a shirt buttoned to the collar beneath a leather jacket that is jangly with old medals. The shirt's too big, but it's nice and clean and pressed. Everest's shirt, I think. And Everest's jacket. And everything else is full K.

Everest carves the chicken, forks the meat onto the plates, the rosemary-onion sauce, the mini lemon wedges. K piles on the rolls and little butter slabs, and Wyatt spoons up some strawberries and sugar. Harvey meows until Wyatt pours her jug of milk into a factory bowl.

"Thinking of everything," she says.

"Your specialty," I tell her.

"Wait," Joseph says, "until you see dessert," and I look at the way he looks at Wyatt, which is the way Grandma Aubrey looks at me, which is a kind of love that maybe there are no good words for, except maybe the look of eternity. All of time inside a splinter of time.

If that makes sense.

It does. To me.

*Someday*, Grandma Aubrey once said, *they will be your family*.

Someday is today, I decide. They came here for us. We're we.

I pull my sweater tight across my chest. The crickets are sawing. The October sun catches in the low clouds. There's the bray of a cow wanting milking. The plates are passed. The lemonade is poured.

"To Grandma Aubrey," Joseph says.

"Here here," says Sam, say the rest of us.

K catches my eye. I catch his. I don't know, exactly, what feeling this is.

We eat the chicken to its bones. We slurp the buttered rolls through the leftover sauce. We taste the sugar strawberries, and we want more and give ourselves more from Wyatt's Tupperware. Overhead a plane steers through the sky, one of the planes from the Muni. Everest starts telling stories about 'Nam— broccoli-top trees and radio panic, napalm and the sergeants and the Hueys that went down tailfirst, and it doesn't matter if Grandma Aubrey is listening eyes-open or listening eyes-closed or even snoring. I keep looking at us, taking a mind picture of us, trying not to think of how this will be just memory one day and not the present moment. My eyes tear up. I swipe the inside of my sweater-elbow past my drippy nose. I think about something Grandma Aubrey once said about how the meaning of life is the stories of life, and right here, I think, is an excellent story.

"Try the cake," Wyatt says now, handing out the utensils and slicing her latest onto the plates. It's a cake built out of berries. It's so tender and sweet I feel my face go red, and then I swallow. Wyatt gives Harvey a little taste. He looks at her with cat eyes. He swishes his tail and jumps up on Grandma Aubrey's lap, and she opens her eyes, and Wyatt says, "Cake?"

"I wouldn't ... miss it," Grandma Aubrey says, breathing hard against the words. "Not for the ... world."

Wyatt deals out a slice.

Grandma Aubrey lifts her fork.

"Oh," she says, and her eyes grow as big as the word.

"We've had some success," Wyatt says now, "locating the hopper's home base."

"Success?" I say.

Grandma Aubrey's eyes grow even bigger. My heart starts beating faster.

"Reconnaissance," K says, which must be a new word for him because he trips the syllables.

Sam puts his plate down, and his fork. He starts to explain the work that's been done "in my absence," as he puts it. By matching the hopper's flight patterns with the aerial maps they've narrowed the number of launch sites of interest.

"How many," I ask, "are of interest?"

"About eight," Sam says. "Call it eight, give or take."

"Eight places where the hopper could take off from or land," I say, for myself and also for Grandma Aubrey. "Eight places where she could have stored her hopper."

"That's right."

"Eight places where maybe she lived."

"Correct."

"Or where somebody lives or works who knows her."

"Eight places to investigate."

"What's next?" Grandma Aubrey says.

"Surveillance," K says.

"We're planning on flying low," Everest says, "in the Cessna."

"Skimming," Sam says.

"We'd take the balloon up, but we can't get close enough to key locales of interest," Joseph says. "Breeze won't take us there. Breeze won't let us hover. So the plane will go up, and we'll look for skid marks and char. We'll see what we can see from there."

"After that," Wyatt says, "there'll be a ground operation. Going door to door. Nobody knows but us. We've kept the secret."

"Avoiding any undue exposure of the facts," Joseph says.

"Avoiding making trouble for the girl, because she's already had so much trouble."

"Too much," Grandma Aubrey says.

"Agreed."

"Reconnaissance," K says the word again.

"So we have our plan," Everest says. "And Sophie here's invited. If that's fine with you, Aubrey. If you're okay letting her go."

"Flying?" Grandma Aubrey says. "Well . . . I am. Of course." She closes her eyes. She leans back. "My Sophie B," she says, "is going flying. It's practically . . . preordained. It's practically . . . the story already written."

"We'll need the right weather," Everest says. "Right time of day. Could be our circumstances interfere with school circumstances. That Wyatt and K here won't be able to join our team."

"Stuck in algebra," K says.

"Or gym." Wyatt rolls her eyes.

"Could be that Sophie will be our best bet, eyes to the ground, eyes on alert. You okay with that, Sophie?"

"Yeah. Sure," I say. "I am."

Except—

I'd be leaving Grandma Aubrey.

I swore I wouldn't leave Grandma Aubrey.

"Wyatt?" I say. "K?" Thinking one or the both of them should save me. Step in. Take on the job so that I can stay on the ground with Grandma Aubrey.

"We can't wait," Wyatt says, "for a good-weather weekend day. The plane has to fly as soon as the weather allows. The clock is ticking on the hopper."

I glance at Joseph. He nods.

I glance at Everest. He's staring at me.

"They won't keep the hopper at the hospital forever," he says. "She's getting stronger, and she'll need to be released. If we don't act fast, chances are we'll lose her to Child Protective Services."

"Or to ICE," Joseph says.

"Or just plain lose her," Wyatt says. And shudders.

"See what we mean?" K says. "We absolutely need you."

He looks into my eyes so long and hard that I feel the heat rise in my cheeks and my own eyes burning.

Wyatt looks up, I look up, we all do. It's like the sky above heard us. On the far side of the horizon a punch of clouds rolls in. The top part is white. The bottom part is gray. The clouds have too much substance.

# TWENTY-SEVEN

THE FIST OF THE CLOUD on the horizon has stayed. Covered up the sky and turned its faucet on. Monday and Tuesday and now—rain or clouds or end-of-October fog. The planes are grounded. Everest's Cessna. The mission. They called me Monday, and they called me Tuesday, and they called me today, first thing.

No planes flying.

The clock is ticking.

In the cottage I take care of family things. I feed the cat. I assist. I fashion up meals that are maybe good enough but wouldn't be good enough if Wyatt were here watching. I do my homeschool schoolwork, by which I mean I read from the stacks of books in Grandma Aubrey's room and from the newspapers and write the things that I think, the lots of things that I think—about headlines and borderlines, about missing strangers and missing people, about namesakes and keepsakes, about the color of K's eyes.

I read the not-private parts out loud. Grandma Aubrey approves or asks for more. She says I should be careful with my grammar and that not every noun wants to be switched into a verb. Then she says, "Poooof, Sophie B, your excellence has . . . tired me." And I say, "You should sleep," and she nods, and she starts snoring. I sit with her, I watch the clock, I do the things best done in silence. By three o'clock in the afternoon, she says she's breathing better, that the worst has passed, that she wants me out of here.

"I'm doing better," she says. "Can't you see?"

Not really.

"You're a kid," she says. "Get . . . going."

"Grandma . . ."

"There's a mission," she says. "And you are on it."

"Planes aren't flying," I say.

"Doesn't matter," she says. "Get down there. Check in. I could use a little solo time."

"You sure?" I say.

"Don't I look sure?" she says. "Seriously, honey. You're getting boring."

She looks like Grandma Aubrey for just this instant. She looks like Grandma Aubrey because she's smiling.

I race the yellow centerline. I lean into the curves, past the farms that are plowed out now, past the cornstalks that are brown, past the cows that aren't so selfish with the shade. By the time I get to the Muni, Wyatt and K are arriving. Off the bus with the lug of their backpacks. I see K when he sees me. He looks away, and he looks back. He is all-out, one-hundred-percent smiling.

He runs, and his backpack thumps.

Wyatt runs, but she can't beat him.

"Sophie B makes an appearance," she says. K says nothing. He doesn't have to.

The rain rains or the clouds cloud. We chase the birds through the Muni tunnels. We sit at the big rolltop desk at the Air Time operation and tidy up the paperwork. We sit on the orange milk crates or the big chair with wheels. We ask each other hopper questions, make hopper speculations, Mauricio Flores speculations, reconnaissance math, trading stories from the news about the kids at the border, the kids without papers, the kids without parents.

We take inventory of the Air Time things: the big bag where the balloon is stuffed, the basket that looks like a wicker gazebo, the bottles of champagne like bowling pins, the giant inflator, the weather on the charts and on the board, the books Joseph reads:

*Taming the Gentle Giant.*

*Hot Air for Pilots.*

And now we're studying the aerial map, the red circles on the map, the places K and Wyatt and the rest of them think the hopper might have been before she went up into the clouds, then fell. The places marked out for our surveillance. For whenever the Cessna can fly, and it has to fly, because we're running out of time.

Wyatt pulls her hair and chews her blue-tipped finger.

K keeps opening the parasail door and coming back holding up his little finger.

"Weather," he says.

He says it just to me.

Wyatt doesn't notice at first, and then she does. She pulls at some of her earrings.

It's raining, and then it's clouds, and then it's fog. We walk back out into the tunnel of Muni planes, their noses sniffing at the hangar air, their propellers like the hands on stopped clocks. Wyatt stretches out her arms, like a cross, and runs, up and down, from the planes toward the waiting lounge, past the plaid chairs and magazines, the posters falling from the walls. She runs yelling what she wishes for—a break in the case, a word from the hopper, the facts as they actually, factually are. The hopper needs a name, and she needs a safe-haven home. She needs an explanation.

She needs us.

The air cracks like bugs are being zapped, and then Wyatt stops, and the air goes quiet, and we head off toward K's old Skyhawk and hang out there, even though there's only really room for one of us. There are birds beneath the plane, pecking at old crumbs. There are gears inside and old magazines and the hand-me-down clothes from the vets. A toothbrush. A towel. A bar of soap. The cracked windshield.

"How do you actually sleep in here?" I ask. Like I used to ask. Like I always will.

K shrugs.

He crushes the hat down on his head.

He looks at Wyatt and then at me beneath his

Frank Sinatra hat. He decides that he has something to say. An actual, factual K story.

"It's not really diamonds that I want, with my wish," he says, and I don't know what he's talking about and then I do, then I remember lying in the grass making summertime wishes. Lying and looking up, when the hopper was magic, when the sky held her up, when the storm wasn't near. "It's chondrites."

"Chondrites?" A word I have not found in any Grandma Aubrey book.

"You don't know about chondrites?" he says. Happy, because he knew I wouldn't.

"No," I say.

"I don't know either," Wyatt says. Biggest gift she could ever give K—Wyatt not knowing something.

She heads off down the tunnel like she doesn't want to hear the story. K and I watch her go, the one side of her black hair flying. A couple of the vets scoot out from underneath their planes and watch. She goes all the way to Air Time. Then she comes back. Pushing the wheely chair from the rolltop desk and two milk crates piled onto the chair.

"Tell us about chondrites," she says. Slightly out of breath. "The whole and factual story."

"Seriously?" K says.

"I'm always serious," Wyatt answers. She's not lying.

K grows an inch or maybe two inches taller. There's no escaping the truth about K: He's the most beautiful boy I'll ever see. I mean that when I say it. I'm not lying.

We take our milk-crate seats. Wyatt takes the chair. K puts his story on display. Chondrites: front and center.

"Chondrites are a straight shot out of time," K begins, a little slow, a little awkward. "Chondrites are like someone took a hammer to the sun and busted it to dust. A chondrite is a cubic crystal. A chondrite is the color of dew. A chondrite really does fall from the sky. Like a diamond would if a diamond could."

"And not like a hopper," Wyatt says. "I guess."

"Chondrite." I repeat the word.

"Chondrite," K says. Sitting there. In his borrowed shirt and his draggy pants and his Sinatra hat beside his Skyhawk. One of the birds jumps up onto his lap. He lets it hop. I bet that bird tickles.

"You want to see a chondrite?" he asks us then.

"You have a chondrite?" Wyatt says.

"My best-kept secret," K says, and Wyatt stops spinning herself on the chair with the wheels, and I lean forward, and K takes off his hat. He slips his fingers into its band. He pulls out what looks like a tiny piece of glass.

"This," he presents, "is my chondrite. Four-point-five-six billion years old. Older than the moon itself. Sulfur. Water. Dust."

He puts the glass thing in my hand.

"You're holding," he goes on, "a piece of the sun. Right there in your hand."

"For real?" Wyatt says, plucking the thing from my open palm and weighing it in her own.

"For real," K says. "My mother called it a tear from the sun."

"For real you never showed me this?"

"I always had it. You never asked."

"Your *mother*?" I say.

"Last thing she said," he says, "when she was dropping me off."

When she was leaving, he means. When she was going away, for good. Taking everything he had, including most of his name. I try to get a picture of the lime green Gremlin in my head. I try to get a picture of his mother, her last wave goodbye. I can't picture her because I can't picture mine. In my head it's blank and empty.

"Your mother gave you this, and then she left, and all this time you had it and you never said—"

I say.

Wyatt also says.

"Having it is good enough," he says. "I'm just showing it to you now."

Wyatt gives a long whistle. I shake my head. We pass the chondrite back and forth, hold it to the light, try to see parts of the sun until K takes it back.

The bird stands on his hand.

The bird flies off.

K slips the thing into the band of his hat.

Crushes the hat back on his head.

I can't take my eyes off that part of him that shines mostly in secret.

We sit there, quiet, listening to the rain on the roof, listening to the birds in the tunnel, listening to the men, listening to the creak of the chair with the wheels when Wyatt starts spinning again, listening to the sound of us not talking to each other.

The biggest distance between two people, Grandma Aubrey always says, is a secret.

"This weather needs to cut it out," Wyatt says, after a long time. "The Cessna has to fly. Every day that goes by without more intel on the hopper is a day we lose," she says.

"Can't get the Cessna up in bad weather," K says.

"'Course not."

"Can't change the weather."

"I know."

"Can't get the hopper to talk, no matter how many blues we bring. Can't find Mr. Flores. Can't know what to do."

"Gotta be *something* we can do," I say. "While we're waiting on the sky." I think some more and then I choose. To get up. To go out. To try.

I stand, and they stand. I walk, and they walk the tunnel of the Muni. Between the planes, in single file. Past the PayDays and the lounge, through the front door. Across the tarmac, past the tower, through the wet, wet fields, into the woods.

I'm out in front.

They follow.

"Maybe there's something we missed out in the woods," I say. "Something from the hopper."

"Okay," Wyatt says, despite the fact that this wasn't her idea.

"Sure," K says, glad to stop the silence.

We crunch through, beneath the trees. We hear the squirrels overhead. We get to the swish of the creek, and then we get to the clearing, where the rain falls down harder. We start hunting for more clues, hopper crash clues. When there's nothing more to say you get up and do something.

We spread out in the crash-site place. We get down on our hands and knees. Wyatt takes the south side, and K takes the north, and I'm off to the west.

I find sticks and busted metal parts. A rim of this. A ring of that. The label off a propane tank. A green bug that looks fluorescent. A fallen nest, like the nest Wyatt found in her kitchen.

"Coming up empty," Wyatt says, from the south.

"Me too," K says from the north. His hair is one big curl. His knees are mud.

"It'll be dark soon," Wyatt says.

I look up. It's hard to tell what the sun is doing when it's raining on your head.

I sweep my hand left and right. I dig. I find an old bird shell. I find a chocolate milk carton. I feel something hard, beneath my hand.

"We should go," K says. He's standing up now, heading my way. I turn around to see him.

Wyatt is standing too, in the hole in the woods, the rain falling on her, this look on her face.

I push the wet dirt away from the thing I've found. I push a little harder. Now here it is, uncovered at last. A silver baby rattle.

"You find something?" Wyatt says.

"I don't know," I say.

"You found something," she says.

I show her what it is.

Her face goes so, so white that I'm afraid she'll faint right here.

"Wyatt?" I say. "You okay, Wyatt?"

K on one side and me on the other, we take her to the moss-log bench.

"What is it, Wyatt?" I say.

"I can't," she says. That's all she says.

We sit with her for as long as she needs.

"Let me see it again," she says now, and I open my hand, and she opens her hand. She takes the silver rattle.

# TWENTY-EIGHT

THURSDAY AFTERNOON: more rain. More Grandma Aubrey insisting that she can't sleep if I stay home. Her words like a broom scooting me out, pushing me on. *Live*, the doctor said, she says. *Live*. Like we are, both of us, patients.

Wyatt isn't talking, but she's baking. Sugar and eggs. Whole milk on the sill. Sea salt, confectioner's snow, an orange already zested. She French whips, and she pours the golden olive oil. Her elbows are shaped like cul-de-sacs. Her arms are skinny. The razored part of her hair is growing out of her scalp and coming in soft as raven feathers, and sometimes— measuring, stiffing, whisking—she lifts her hand and strokes the feathers back into their places and closes her eyes and says nothing.

Slips the cake into the oven.

K's somewhere, I don't know where. Protecting himself, maybe, from Wyatt's mood, which has stayed this mucky since yesterday, when I found and then she took the rattle. Wouldn't let it go. Needed help heading back. Didn't run ahead. Didn't follow.

"Wyatt," I say. "Can you just tell me one thing?"

"One thing?"

"About the rattle?"

She looks at me. She shakes her head. It's a question she won't answer.

"There'll be crystals of salt in the wet wish of this cake," she says. "And lemon and also orange zest far out on the edge."

"Sounds excellent," I say.

"Hopper Blues," she says.

"I know," I say. "But—"

"We must," she says, "preserve our focus. Our focus is the hopper."

"Fine," I say.

"Fine," she says. "They've got her in Therapy," Wyatt says. "Did I tell you that?"

About a thousand times, she's told me. All those days when Wyatt and K went and I couldn't. All this week too—Wyatt getting her updates from Joseph who gets his updates from Nurse Cara. It's been awhile since Wyatt herself has gone to see the hopper.

Today we're going, and Wyatt won't talk about the rattle. Today I'll see the hopper for the first time in a long time, and maybe she won't remember me. I'm excited, but I'm worried, but that's not all: Wyatt has a secret. It concerns a baby's rattle.

"She and Nurse Cara are learning to quilt," Wyatt says. "Nurse Cara learns and then teaches the hopper, and the hopper's a good quilter."

"You mentioned," I say.

"They're working her out on machines. Treadmills and things. Therapy."

"You said."

"Just getting you ready. Fixing expectations. Our hopper is not the same hopper."

"Thanks," I say, but what I'd like to say is, *What's with you, Wyatt? What's with you, and why won't you tell me?*

K swings through the factory door. He wears a navy blue rain jacket that falls so far past his knees you could say it stops at his ankles.

"We ready?" he says.

"Waiting on the bake," Wyatt says.

He doesn't ask her about the rattle.

"Fog is thick," K says. "Clouds are too heavy for the sky."

"Doesn't mean we're not going," Wyatt says.

"Of course," K says. "I didn't say that."

I shrug when Wyatt isn't looking.

K shrugs back.

# TWENTY-NINE

WYATT'S OUT IN FRONT with her cake in her basket and her canvas bag strapped to her back, her flashlight on. We're riding safe, near the shoulder of the road. Riding through fog like this is like swimming in the sea, the one time I swam inside the sea, which was a long time ago when I was a kid and when Grandma Aubrey still had sprite in her legs and a bathing suit that fit.

I feel my hair slick back. I feel the puddle spray. On the next long turn I take the lead, feel Wyatt's light behind me.

"You go on ahead . . . or . . . you'll make me mad," Grandma Aubrey said when I left this afternoon. "How am I going to dream my dreams if you are here to . . . watch . . . me."

I gave her a shhh. I gave her a kiss. I'm thinking of her, and we're riding.

I almost miss the sign to the road that the hospital's on, but I don't. I turn, K and Wyatt turn, we splatter through the fog and through the puddles. No bikes in the rack, but now there are ours. The lady with the owl glasses smiles when the fog pushes us in.

"Looks like you're carrying the weather," she says. She nods at Wyatt's plastic-wrapped box and waves us in.

Our shoes and our boots and our coats squeak down the hall. We leave a trail behind us.

The hopper is not in her room. The jar for flowers has fresh new flowers. A stuffed pig is half asleep on the hospital pillow. A fresh hospital gown waits by the pig. There's a basket on the floor with quilting scraps and threads and needles. The hopper must be, K says, down the hall, so that's where we head— down the hall and down the next hall, to Therapy. The colors of the walls change from green to blue. Therapy's at the end.

Sign says it.

K points.

He goes first. Side by side, Wyatt and I follow, and Wyatt gives me a look, and I catch it. I don't know the name for it because the look doesn't say only one thing. The look says *here we go and what will happen? and we don't have much more time and I'm sorry I've been a jerk about the rattle* all in the exact same precise moment.

Therapy is a yellow room, bright as sun, with machines and balls and weights and pulleys. "Like a gym," Wyatt had said, when she'd explained it. The hopper's standing up like K had shown she'd started standing, with her legs a little crooked and far apart. She's wearing gray sweatpants and a sorority T-shirt, which is probably a hand-me-down, by which I mean it's probably Nurse Cara's. Her back's to us, but Nurse Cara sees us square. She sits in a plastic chair along the wall, watching the hopper working.

She waves. We wave back. There's room beside her, in other plastic chairs. We sit and watch, another hopper show. There are mirrors on two walls. There are charts of bones and muscles. Scales. The hopper's face is one hundred percent concentrated. It's like there's nothing in her thoughts except her legs.

We sit real quiet.

"Just keep walking," the Therapy guy says. His name is Mike, according to the pin on his shirt. A shirt that is too small for all his muscles.

"Exactly," he says, encouraging. "Yes," he says. "Keep going."

The hopper's hair has gotten longer since before. She's taller than I thought she'd be, standing up like that. She doesn't see us, and then she does, reflected in the mirror. She startles.

"Don't stop," Mike says.

She doesn't stop.

"I thought she spoke Spanish," I whisper to Wyatt.

"Everybody knows how encouragement *sounds*," she says. "Doesn't matter which words you use, which language."

Nurse Cara asks me how I've been. Says she's missed seeing me around. Says she's at the end of her shift, just hanging out, likes to watch the progress of the hopper. She tells me about the quilt they're making. How many squares they've got in. How many colors. Then she asks again how I have been. Says she's missed seeing me around.

I tell her about Grandma Aubrey.

"MS," I say.

"Wyatt mentioned," she said. "MS is hard."

I nod. I watch the hopper.

"She won't see a doctor," I say. "She says she already knows how to live."

"K says she's a balloon aficionado," Nurse Cara says.

"Sounds like K," I say. Sniffing a little.

"Everest says she's a lot like you."

"Really?" I say. "Everest says that?"

I think about Grandma Aubrey with her Einstein hair and her oxford shirts and her shortness. I think about me, who looks nothing like that. And her in her bed. And me here with my friends.

"A real family resemblance," Nurse Cara says.

"Well," I say. "That's nice."

Mike moves the hopper to a new machine he calls the stepper. He dials a dial. He sets things up. She climbs aboard and starts to step, one step rotating pushing down upon another. This is a hard one. I can see the hardness of it crawling into her skin. Up her narrow neck past her chin into her cheeks. Her dark eyes catch mine in the mirror.

"You're doing great," I try to get my eyes to say.

Wyatt gives her a high-five sign.

K points to Wyatt's cake. "Sweet reward coming," he says.

Wyatt sticks her elbow in his side. "Let her focus, K," she says.

"Is she in pain?" Nurse Cara asks me. "Your Grandma Aubrey?"

"Probably. She is. Yeah. But she doesn't talk about it."

"Could she use some help?"

"I help," I say. But then I think how I'm here and not there and how Grandma Aubrey says that my number one job is being a kid and finding my joy because my joy is her joy, and that when I stay home I bore her—she honestly swears it. Is that helping? I don't see how. I am here with my friends. She's alone in her bed. Alone with Harvey. Swearing that she's better, but I know what's true: she's faking.

"Of course you do. But there are things that can be done to ease—"

The hopper looks a little tilty on the stepper, like she could lose her balance. Mike stops the machine and reaches for her hand. He says something we can't hear. She catches her breath.

Looks me in the eyes. Again.

I want to tell Nurse Cara about the Sunday picnic. About everybody coming. About how Grandma

Aubrey rallied for the afternoon, but after that she rattled and rattled, breathed so hard I thought she'd tear a hole straight through her lungs. About how she snored pretty bad when she slept, and I wished the snoring would stop, but when it stopped it was worse than when it was going. And how I almost called 911 but didn't because I didn't want to upset my Grandma Aubrey.

And then how, more and more, she made me leave the cottage.

"I'll be a heap of depressed if you don't go out and be a kid," she'd say.

"But—" I'd say.

"I'm the boss."

I want to tell that story, but it's a long story, and now Mike is telling the hopper that their session is coming to an end. That she's done great work for the day, does she feel herself getting stronger? The hopper nods like she understands. Mike helps her off the stepper. He helps her to her walker. He helps her walk her way to us. The heat's still in her cheeks. The lights from the room are in her eyes. We're in her eyes too. She smiles.

"Look what we've brought," Wyatt says.

She pops the lid on her cake box. Puts the cake on her chair. Pulls a knife from her bag and knives in. Cuts a slice for all of us and the thickest slice for the hopper. She has a roll of paper towels in her bag. The paper towels become our napkins.

"I knew that if I hung out here after work I'd get lucky," Nurse Cara says. She stands and helps the hopper into the seat where she's been sitting. Wyatt hands her her slice. She doesn't eat until the hopper eats. Until she can see the expression on her face.

"I knew it," Wyatt says. "I knew you'd like it."

The hopper almost laughs. The hopper, I think, is pretty. An old man in a wheelchair is wheeling in, and Wyatt cuts another couple of slices. One for Mike and one for the man.

"I was hoping," Mike says, "that you wouldn't forget me."

"So what about our hopper," Nurse Cara says, as she's finishing her slice. There are crumbs on the lap of her mint green pants and more crumbs on the speckled tiles beneath us.

"Doing so well," I say.

"Yeah," Wyatt says.

"Almost ready for the real world," K says, and

now all the light in the hopper's eyes go dark, and she looks away, and Nurse Cara gets up to get something for the hopper, leaves the room. And now Mike is wheeling Mr. Wheelchair. No adults are watching. Zero chaperone.

Wyatt gives us the shhh look, and we wait to be sure that we have our break. We wait to take the minute that is ours. I think about what the clerk in the Docs store said about the man the hopper had come with. I think about the crumpled dollar bills. No credit card. No address. Just the name written on the bird: Mauricio Flores.

Nurse Cara's gone. Mike is distracted. I stand, then I kneel. I face the hopper.

"I've got a house," I say, "not far from here. If you need somewhere to stay. After this."

"And I've got a house," Wyatt says.

"And I've got a Skyhawk," K says.

"You don't have to be afraid," I say. "That's all that we're saying."

The hopper's eyes say a thousand different things.

"We're your friends," I say.

"We want to help you," Wyatt says.

"Just talk to us," K says. "Tell us something."

"Mauricio Flores," I say, and the hopper's eyes go even bigger, and Wyatt slips her hand into one of her pockets, slides the bird onto her palm. She makes sure the hopper sees, and the hopper sees—her eyes so big and startled.

"Ana Celeste?" the hopper says after a long, long time.

The shout of her name as a question.

# THIRTY

ALL NIGHT I LIE AWAKE on my bed, thinking about the hopper and the sound of her shout, listening to Grandma Aubrey snoring. Every breath she takes sounds like her last. And then there's silence. And then I worry. And then she starts again, and I think again about the hopper. Ana Celeste. Her name. At last. Ana Celeste, and that's all she said, and Wyatt slipped her the origami bird, and she took the bird. She put it somewhere safe, where no one could see, so no one could ask her.

Harvey goes in between the rooms. When the sun begins to rise he's in the shadows.

My fat cat.

My Harvey.

The hopper's name is Ana Celeste. The hopper talks. She trusts us. All we'd ever needed was time alone. Kid to kid. Kid secrets.

"If you're afraid to go back home," Wyatt had said, "we understand."

"If someone's hurting you—" K said.

The hopper had shaken her head.

"If—" Wyatt said.

And then Nurse Cara returned, and we stood and said goodbye. Left the rest of the cake with the hopper, said hello to the doctor in the hall who passed us by, rode back through the fog that was turning into dusk, but still the fog was lifting, and we thought we'd broken through, we thought we'd built the bridge, we thought we had saved the day, but Joseph got a call.

Joseph got a hospital reprimand.

Joseph got word: we weren't to return to the hopper.

We'd upset her.

We'd interfered.

We'd said something and she could not be consoled.

We weren't to return to the hopper.

"But we were helping," Wyatt said, insisted on it, her voice all tears.

"But we were getting close," K said.

"She told us her name," I said. "And we gave her Mauricio Flores. We're the ones," I said. "We're the ones—"

And Joseph said, "Rules are rules, and we were already bending rules. The hospital isn't budging."

Now the sun comes in. The sun. No rain. No weather. Through the morning haze, I hear the phone ringing.

"Sophie," Grandma Aubrey calls, her voice crackling. "It's Everest. They need . . . you. At the Muni."

I'm pulling on my jeans, my shirt, my sweater. I'm pulling a brush through my hair, using the Ladies. I'm putting the hot water on for Grandma Aubrey's tea. Pouring milk into a bowl for Harvey. I peel the skin from a pink grapefruit. I get a squirt of the sour in my eye.

"Are you sure?" I say now, by my grandma's side. "You'll be all right?"

"I will be angry," Grandma Aubrey says, "If you don't . . . get . . . going."

Harvey takes a leap up onto her bed.

"You're in charge," I say. And kiss them.

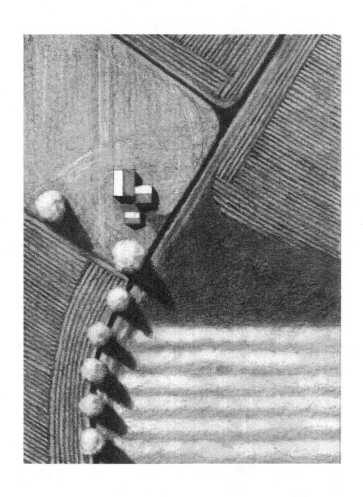

# THIRTY-ONE

THE EARTH FROM THE SKY is pinwheels and donkeys. The earth from the sky is road ribbons and streams and autumn colors and autumn leaves. I see the curve of our shadow on the silos and horses, the mountain dog in the fenced-in yard, the mowed skirts of farms, the yellow tick lines marking roads, the girl on roller skates. I see the two steeples of the white church Grandma Aubrey says we'll visit sometime and the flat stones of a graveyard and another dribble of a creek. I see something spark inside the suds of trees and the horizontal shine in windowpanes and the black cows in the blue mist. I see, and all this beauty's got me whipped.

"Air's just right," Everest says, in the Cessna cockpit beside me. "Easy does it."

Our headphones are on. Our gear.

The map is on my lap. The red circles of maybe.

Everest has his 'Nam jacket on and his flying cap, and his white hair is even whiter than Grandma Aubrey's. But his face is so young, and his eyes are sky blue, and there's a smile on his face because he's flying.

Finally flying.

Weather all clear.

The ping of sun on a metal roof. The run of sun on the neon sign of the Twenty Four. Smoke rising from some chimneys and school buses in a lot and the school where K and Wyatt go, but I've never been and don't know if I will ever be, and all the friends they have or don't have, the stories that go on without me. Everything down there seen from up here.

Time stops, but the air moves.

The land moves.

The plane rumbles. The noise is its own kind of silence, and besides, Everest and I don't need much talk. We know what we're looking for as we fly the low sky, and I am ready with my pen and the clipboard that we borrowed from Air Time.

"Good luck, Sophie," Sam had said, unwrapping the scarf from around his neck and wrapping it around mine as we stood there on the runway.

"You take care of her now," Joseph had said, as Everest revved the engine, squinted at the prospects. Then Joseph had given me a hug and slipped me a note from Wyatt, also a piece of blueberry sugar candy.

YOU'RE THE BEST ONE FOR THE JOB, Wyatt's note said, and then K had signed it too, the single letter that is a big reaching letter, with its two strong arms and one spine.

I'd put the words in my jacket pocket, along with a good-luck charm from Grandma Aubrey, and now beyond the shake of the plane the birds holler. Down below the dogs run. All the rain from the week before is soaking in, though some of it is still inside gutters, buckets, trees.

"Here we go," Everest says. "Prospect one."

He descends. I feel the rumble in my knees. He checks the map and points to where we're going. I look out, then down, and see. We're headed to the chain of hills, on the edge. There's the bump of the earth and a deep ravine, hawks and turkey vultures flying on thermals. I see a small road climb the hill and then a place where the hill flattens out, and there, on the flat, is a house in two parts. Or a house, I see, and its garage.

When he'd studied this map Sam had plunked his thumb right here, put a little smudge on the spot.

"Plenty of room," he'd said "for a hopper operation. And a nice little elevation to give her a hopping start."

The Cessna flies and the earth moves. Everest tells me the names of the gadgets and dials—the air speed indicator and the compass and the GPS and the altimeter and the portable collision avoidance system, and there's more but I'm losing track, and now we start to bank, take a turn, see what can be seen. I get a little dizzy and remember Wyatt's words.

*I am the one for this job.*

I remember K's K.

"Looks abandoned, all right," Everest says, through his microphone, into my headphones.

The closer we get the better I see the rusted barrels lined up out front by the road, the bent neck of the mailbox, the broken shutters on the house, the cracked glass in the garage door. The working theory on prospect one was that the hopper hopped out of here because no one would suspect her. That she'd hauled her machinery up the hill and tucked it in the empty garage and taken advantage of the hill.

But there's no sign that anyone has been here at all, not for many years. No flattened grass where she'd hop up from or hop down. No sign of the inflator fan that she'd need to start her trick. *They blow the balloon up with a fan*, Joseph had told me. *Just like we do here at Air Time.* She'd never returned after she took that tragic hop. The inflator fan would still be outside, unless someone on the ground had helped her get up, then pulled the inflator fan inside. But who would help a hopper fly out into a storm?

"That would be like sending someone out on a suicide mission," Sam said, when he considered and then dismissed the possibility. "That would be—"

"Criminal," Joseph finished.

"Nothing but nothing down there," I say now, and Everest nods.

I write the facts on my clipboard page. Everest banks as we head off to prospect two. There are school buses on the Gilbertine roads. Wyatt and K somewhere down there with their backpacks on, with the other kids they hardly talk about, the kids I never see. And now the Twenty Four and the field where we slept, Grandma Aubrey and me, during our first night after our long ride, when we'd left the blue valley behind.

"You'll always have the valley," Grandma Aubrey said that night in the truck, "tucked inside your memory. Close your eyes, and you'll always find what you need inside your dreams."

She closed her eyes to show me what she meant. She held my hand and squeezed it.

"See?"

But I kept my eyes open, watching the stars. The silver freckles of the sky. I kept my eyes open wondering what would happen next. I never dreamed the blueberries. I never dreamed the Muni. I never dreamed Wyatt and K and the Vietnam vets. I never dreamed that I would see the earth from the sky not secondhand through a book but firsthand through my eyes.

Or that there'd be a hopper.

Or that Grandma Aubrey would stop leaving her bed. Would only see the floaters she loved through her open window.

"Prospect two," Everest says, and I check the map and check the view. I see what he sees. Down below is a grass parking lot. Beside the lot is a concrete square with a flat-topped roof and through the roof grow a garden of weeds.

"Joey's Old Repair Shop," Everest says. He flies overhead then circles back. We take in the view from both directions.

"What do you see?" he asks.

"Don't see much," I say.

No fan, no skid marks, no flattened grass.

"Joey died five years ago," Everest says. "He was one of us."

"From the Muni?"

"A vet. Went a little crazy in the end. When he did we didn't see him much. He just shacked up there. And died."

"Sounds bad," I say.

"The war," he says, "was hard on all of us. It was hard on all of us, different."

Everest flies again and flies over. We circle back. His skin looks bruised beneath his eyes. He squints. Tugs on his hat.

"Don't see signs of the hopper out there, do you?"

"I do not," I say.

He flies on.

I make my notes on the page on the clipboard.

Over the Twenty Four again and now over the Muni, the three hangar huts glistening in the sun, the rows of Wyatt's blues, the factories, the house where Wyatt lives with Joseph Bell, for almost, I guess, her whole life. But not her whole life. Wyatt's life didn't start at the Muni. Wyatt's life is the question I've always known, from basically day one, that I had no business asking.

Actually, factually, don't ask her.

Prospect three is an old warehouse, and here again there is no sign of hopper activity. Prospect four is a graveyard with a caretaker's shed; the graveyard's only history now, and a field of grass where no graves were dug, and definitely no signs of the hopper, which is a relief because I think that's creepy, the idea of stepping into and out of the sky on the bones of dead people. The sun has moved to a different place within the sky. It comes in as a slice through the cockpit window, and I close my eyes, feel the turn of the plane, feel us banking when I look up again, look down on the red blare of a siren. It's an ambulance driving the curve of the road between the cows I know best and the green. An ambulance on the road between the Muni and the cottage.

"Everest?" I say, but I don't need to say it because he's seen what I've seen, he's calling something in to the Muni, numbers and abbreviated things. Ten-four. He's flying just overhead and opposite to the ambulance and its siren, and now we're over and see something else—someone behind the ambulance on a Harley.

"Everest?"

"Aborting reconnaissance," Everest is saying to the ground crew at the Muni. "Coming in for a quick landing."

"Faster," I say. "Faster. Please."

# THIRTY-TWO

JOSEPH'S WAITING ON THE MUNI DRIVE in Everest's pickup, my Schwinn already tossed in the back and the truck motor on. Everest touches down, brakes, opens the hatch, and I jump out, Everest does, Sam climbs in to finish up the Cessna's business, and now Everest and I are into the truck, and Joseph stays at the wheel, and I've never been down this road so fast. I've never seen everything we're passing so full of blur. I don't count the miles, I don't count the minutes, I don't say a word.

Then Joseph does.

"She had a spell, Sophie," he says. "Just a spell. Don't worry."

"You talked to her?"

"I talked to them. Your grandma is fine."

"There is an ambulance at my house," I say. "With its sirens on."

"Precautionary," he says. "I've been over everything with the EMTs."

The farms and the barns and the autumn colors. Everything we saw from up above.

"Hurry," I say. "Please."

Until we're off the road onto the cottage drive and the wheels of the truck are crunching the pebbles. Everest opens his door, jumps out, and lets me run first. "Grandma Aubrey!" I call. "I'm coming!" Up the porch steps and across the porch and through the screen door past Harvey.

A woman in khaki pants and black boots and a gray shirt steps out into the hallway from my grandma's room. She has reddish hair, green eyes, Irish freckles, and three horizontal forehead lines.

"That is my grandma, and I am Sophie," I say, hard and rushed.

"Sure," she says. "Joseph called ahead. Your grandma's fine."

She is not fine, I think. Fine is not an ambulance. Fine is not an EMT. Fine is not a reconnaissance cut short, with Everest and Joseph beside me.

I turn the corner into her room and find her there—a leather bag on her bed, a blood pressure cuff around her arm, a tube running up into her nose, and a green tank beside her. A guy maybe five years older than me is overseeing the remaining operation. There's a stretcher on the floor, some towels, a glass of water, and somebody's closed the windows.

"She'll catch a chill," the ambulance lady says. I must be staring at the windows. Now I stare at Grandma Aubrey.

She breathes.

Her eyelids flutter.

She raises one hand to say hi. She tries to talk, but her words come out like a wheeze.

"I'll do the talking," the ambulance lady says.

Everest and Joseph are watching, standing in the doorway.

"Your grandma's fine," the lady repeats.

"That's what you said," I say. "That's what everybody's said. She doesn't look so fine to me."

"Fine for now," the lady says. "Fine for the time being."

Grandma Aubrey gives me her *watch your manners* look. She doesn't have to talk for me to know what she's thinking.

"Sorry," I say.

"She had a little scare. She fell. Getting to the bathroom. A lucky fall."

"How would that be lucky?" I say, and I think, Why was she going to the bathroom? Why didn't she use the bedpan? Why didn't she wait for me? Because I was coming. I'd always be coming. I'll always be here for Grandma Aubrey. Almost.

"If she was going to fall she fell in just the right spot. Close enough to the phone. Close enough to call us."

I try to picture that. Picture Grandma Aubrey getting up. Picture her falling. Picture her crawling to the phone and dialing. Hands and knees. Messed-up muscles. Lungs that barely breathe. Maybe it hurt and she was scared. Maybe she called the Muni and no one answered. Maybe she thought that if she was back in bed before I got home I wouldn't guess that something happened. Grandma Aubrey and her pride and her knowing how upset I'd be if I found her hurting.

"So she's okay," I say, my tone a little softer.

"No broken bones."

"Just a scare?"

"Sophie, you understand that your grandma's sick, don't you?"

"I live here," I say. "With her."

"MS is progressive. Her MS is progressing. Her muscles and her joints aren't behaving like they should. Have you heard of myelin, Sophie? The myelin sheath? It wraps itself around the nerves. It's there as a protection. But in MS, the sheath is under attack by the body's immune system, and in late-stage MS, the situation gets worse. The muscles cramp. They spasm. They can't be trusted."

"I know about MS," I say.

"I'm sure you do. I'm sorry. But this, today, was a lucky day. This was a fall and nothing got broken, and she's back in bed where she should be. But there's only so much luck in cases like your grandma's. Her lungs will need more oxygen than her lungs can give her, Sophie. Her body needs good care. She needs a proper care facility."

"This is very proper," I say. "We are."

"That's not what I mean. I mean—"

"I know what you mean."

"How long have you lived in Gilbertine?"

"More than a year."

"When's the last time your grandma saw a doctor?"

"Since before that."

"That isn't," the ambulance lady says, trying to collect the right words, "how it's supposed to be."

Joseph and Everest are still there, in the doorway. Harvey's gone away and come back. I look at Grandma Aubrey, pillowed up in her white bed in her white sheets with her white hair and her white nightshirt, the cuff on her arm, the tube in her nose. She shakes her head, *no no no*, and I know without her saying a thing that she will not go in for care, she will not move again to die, she will not leave her cottage or her fat cat or me because her living's here.

"She—" I start.

"Wasn't going ... to the bathroom," Grandma Aubrey interrupts. "Was going to ... the window."

"To the window?" the ambulance lady says.

"To see."

Grandma Aubrey points toward the October breeze beyond the glass. To the farm beyond, the autumn colors. The ambulance lady and guy look at one another quick as if suddenly it occurs to them that they don't know everything.

"To see what?" the lady says.

"Sophie," Grandma Aubrey says. "Was ... flying. I had to see."

"You got up to go to the window?" The ambulance lady says, writing this down in a pad she'd had stuffed in her shirt. "Not to the bathroom."

"That's right."

"You couldn't just stay in bed and watch from there?"

"No," Grandma Aubrey says. "I could not."

"It mattered that much?"

"Yes. It did."

"Either way," the lady says. "You fell."

"I did."

"You called."

"You came. And for that . . . I'm grateful. For all your . . . help. Thank you. But—"

"You should take this as a sign," the guy says. "A sign of what's to come. You'll need to get some help going forward. You'll need to take precautions, like Sandy says."

"No," Grandma Aubrey says. "No. I cannot. I am sorry."

She takes a deep breath in and a deep breath out. The oxygen in her nose is relieving.

"We are very grateful," Joseph says, "for your help this afternoon. For your caring."

"We go where we're called," the lady says.

"But I think you can see—" Everest says.

"That it's a lot for one day," Sandy says.

"That. Yes," Joseph says. "We'll take things from here."

"We'll need to file a report," Sandy says.

"We understand."

"Social Services will be checking in."

"Everyone," Joseph says, "has a job."

"Right now I think we all just need to catch our breath," Everest says, stepping forward. "So if you could—"

The ambulance guy starts packing. The case. The stretcher. The cuff. He leaves the tube in Grandma Aubrey's nose and the green tank where it is.

"We'll supply you with extra tanks," he says. "You'll need them."

"You are . . ." Grandma Aubrey says. "So kind."

"These are the instructions," Sandy says, pulling a brochure out of the case. "Oxygen management."

I take the brochure. I thank her.

"There's a number to call for resupplies. They deliver."

"We'll leave two extra tanks by the front door," the guy says. "After that—"

"We understand," Joseph says. "We'll see it through."

The guy bends down to touch Harvey on the head. He salutes Everest and Joseph. "My grandfather," he says, "was in 'Nam. He kept a plane down there, at the Muni. Beat-up Skyhawk."

"The Skyhawk?" I say.

"Never fixed it. Never flew it. Just liked having it around," the guy says.

"You must be Jackson's grandson," Joseph says, after a minute of remembering.

The guy brightens. "Yeah. I am. You knew him?"

"Served with him. Honorable guy."

"Yeah?"

"Yeah. He was. And how he loved that Skyhawk. Loved her just like she was."

"Give the Skyhawk my regards," the guy says, and my heart bumps.

"Come down and visit," Joseph says. "Anytime."

"Will do."

"Thank you. For coming."

Joseph shakes the guy's hand. Everest salutes him. They shake Sandy's hand too, and now they step aside so that the two can pass.

"Take care of yourself, Aubrey," Sandy says. "And remember—"

"I remember."

"Sophie," Sandy says. "Make the right choices."

We hear their boots in the hall, then the screen door. Then the ambulance crunches the pebbles on the drive and rolls down the road, away.

Grandma Aubrey runs her fingers through her hair.

"So much . . . commotion," she says. "I'm so . . . sorry."

"Nothing to be sorry for," I say. "I'm just glad that you're okay."

Though she's not okay. I know she's not okay. She hasn't been for a long time.

I take off my boots. I keep my coat on. I open the window, let the breeze in, climb into bed beside Grandma Aubrey, pull the blanket to her chin, careful around the lines of oxygen, the green canister. Joseph and Everest talk low to each other, then Everest heads down the hall for the extra oxygen tanks and then comes back and gives me instructions.

"You understand?" he says. "How it works?"

"It's not that hard," I say.

"Funny about the guy and the Skyhawk," Joseph says.

"Wait," I say, "until you tell K." But I want to tell K. I want to go back to the Muni just like my Grandma Aubrey is A-okay, but she is not, she has not been for such a very long time, A-okay. She has been holding on for my sake, and now she's trying to let me go. She told me to fly, and I flew. I should have listened to the other voice inside myself.

Joseph stands beside Everest. Neither one leaves.

"Okay, then," Joseph finally says. "We'll go. We'll check in later in the day."

"Okay."

"If you need anything—"

"Could you tell Wyatt and K?" I say. "Could you tell them I'm sorry we didn't finish up the recon?"

"We'll finish it up. Don't worry."

"Everest?"

"Yes?"

"Thank you for the ride."

"You are an excellent copilot."

"Except we didn't find anything."

"We eliminated prospects," Everest says. "An essential part of the process."

"You know what I mean."

"There's still time."

"Not that much of it," I say.

# THIRTY-THREE

"SOPHIE?" GRANDMA AUBREY SAYS. It's dark outside. The air is chill.

"Yeah?"

"Tell me . . . everything."

The paper balloons that hang from the ceiling are bobbing on the breeze. The bowl of soup that I warmed for her is sitting on the floor. Harvey's somewhere else, and twice already Wyatt's called me from the Muni.

"She okay?" she asked the first time.

"She's here," I said.

"You okay?"

I didn't answer.

"K says hi. K says he's sorry."

"Tell K hi. Tell him—"

"What, Sophie?"

"Nothing," I say.

And for once Wyatt knew not to ask any more questions.

*Make a wish*, Wyatt said.

I wish not for this, and nobody needs for me to say it. Nobody needs for me to say how scared I am, how sad I am, how I don't know what I would do if they took Grandma Aubrey somewhere else, if she left us, if she left me.

Except she's here to live.

Except she's dying.

Except there's nothing we can do about it.

MS is mean. It takes things from you. It will take her from me.

"Sophie?"

"Shhh," I say.

"Just . . . tell . . . a story."

But you can't fix everything with a story. You can't pretend that the thing that's happening right now isn't the most important story. Because you don't know how it's going to end. Because you don't know who you'll be when it is ending. Because you don't know how you'll know that it is ending.

"It'll help, dear," she says.

"Please," she says.

I close my eyes. I dig in deep. I make the story of right now the story I can tell Grandma Aubrey. I tell her about the sky. I tell her about the earth from above, which is like the book, I say, only the book in moving pictures. I tell her about cutting through clouds and swooping over chimneys. About how you slide when you bank, and you try to hang on, but in the sky there is nothing to hold onto.

"Oh," she says. "That's lovely."

"Yeah. But also kind of scary."

She starts to cough. I rub her back. I pull the blankets to her chin. Two blankets now, and soon I'll get another.

"We'll never close the windows again," she said, earlier today. "Not while I'm in charge."

But it's cold. And she feels it. I feel it.

"What else?" she says.

"We couldn't find proof of the hopper," I say. "When we were up there. We turned up nothing."

"If only I hadn't—"

"No."

"If—"

"It's okay."

"I wanted to see you . . . flying."

"I know."

"And . . . I did see you. I waved. You were up . . . there. So exciting. You'll fly again," she says. "Tomorrow."

Tomorrow, I think, I won't be flying. Tomorrow or Sunday Everest will take K or Wyatt up. And they'll look down and try to see the start of the hopper's story. Ana Celeste is her name, but that's all she'll say. She'll be leaving the hospital soon, but no one's come to claim her, and all this time we thought we could save her. The girl who flew into a storm on purpose. The girl whose story we've tried to find. The girl who's kept it from us.

"I found a rattle," I say now, "out in the woods. Out in the hole in the trees where the hopper fell."

"Hmmm," Grandma Aubrey says.

"It was smooshed pretty deep in, was pretty muddy."

"Hmmm."

"I guess all the rain helped me dig it up. Brought it closer to the surface, but I don't get it."

"Get what, Sophie?"

"What the hopper was doing with a rattle. Why she'd carry that up to the clouds."

"Hmmm," Grandma Aubrey says. "Yes."

"Or why Wyatt, when I showed her, got so upset she nearly fainted."

"Did she . . . now?"

"She did."

"What did she say?"

"She wouldn't. Say."

The stars are out there. November is soon. I need to get up and find the other blanket. I need to be sure I'm doing the oxygen right, that I read the gauge, that I switch the can out, that I keep my grandma breathing.

"K has a chondrite," I say now. "He says it fell from the sky."

"Oh my," Grandma Aubrey murmurs.

"Keeps it tucked into his hat. It was his secret."

"Isn't that nice."

"It's not his secret anymore."

"Secrets," Grandma Aubrey says, "are better shared."

And I know that's right and true. I know that's true for Grandma Aubrey. She has given me all that she's loved. She has not wasted one single secret. All she's ever wanted in return is stories. My stories. Sky stories. To see the earth from up above. To give me the life she might have had, here in Gilbertine.

I am named for Grandma Aubrey's hero.

That makes Grandma Aubrey a hero to me.

"Aren't we living now?" she sometimes asks me, when I Schwinn back from the Muni with Wyatt's jam-a-lade, with stories that I tell her, Muni stories, 'Nam stories, stories about the floaters. "Yes," she says. "We are living."

I am.

But living is this too, I guess. Living is living beside your Grandma Aubrey when your Grandma Aubrey's dying.

"You know Sophie Blanchard?" she says now. "The . . . original?"

I smirk. "What do you think?"

"You know how she died?"

"I know," I say.

"You tell that story."

"Her dying story?"

"You tell that now. I want to hear it."

I don't start because I don't want to. She squeezes my hand. She insists.

"Like you told it to me?" I say.

"The very same," she says.

I pause again.

I begin.

"July 16, 1819," I say. "The Jardin de Tivoli. Music and sky and crowds. The big Madame Blanchard show is starting, and the air inside her balloon is hot and full of itself, and it is ready."

"Aaahh, yes," she says. "It's ready."

"Weight's off, they say. She's up," I say. "In her white gown and her plumes, with her feathers flapping. She's up one hundred feet, two hundred feet, five hundred feet, and the balloon is rising, and the crowd is watching, and up and up goes Madame Blanchard, the world's greatest balloon artist, and the crowd roars, the crowd cheers. She is their star."

"Forty-one years old," Grandma Aubrey says. "More at ease in the air than with the . . . earth at her feet."

"She is rising," I say. "She is above and the earth is spreading out beneath her, the fog and the people and the city. High, she goes. And higher."

"Lovely."

"And she is up, and she is up, and now it's time."

"For the Bengal lights."

"For the show. Madame Sophie Blanchard lights her rockers. She flicks them out, like she's tossing flowers, only the flowers are flames, they're firework spectaculars. They light the sky. They boom. They fizz. The crowd goes crazy down below. Red. Hot. White. Blue. Orange. Sizzle. The sky is full of color."

"Her sky."

"Her sky. Yes. The sky belongs to Madame Sophie Blanchard."

I stop. I don't like the rest of it. I don't want to say it. Because this is the great Sophie Blanchard's final flight. Her great balloon's on fire.

"Go on," Grandma Aubrey says.

"I can't." I feel the tears in my eyes, on my cheeks.

"The story is that she was doing . . . what she loved," Grandma Aubrey says. "The story is that she . . . was living."

"But then she died," I say. "It was her last, her final ride."

"We will all . . . die," Grandma Aubrey says. "But not until our last and final moment." She puts her hand over mine this time. She squeezes it as hard as her dying muscles let her.

"I don't want you to go," I say, and now I can't stop sobbing.

"I don't want . . . to go, either. Last thing I want is . . . to go. But when I do go, Sophie B, I will . . . leave you everything we did and everything we found and every adventure that we went on and all my love. And you will always have our everything. In the sky. Beyond."

I rest my head against her shoulder. I feel the muscle twitch within.

I have this.

I have it now.

I'll have it for as long as I do.

# THIRTY-FOUR

I DON'T GO ANYWHERE NOW, except to the store for Grandma Aubrey, for the soft things she can eat, for the sauce and soup and ice cream that is easiest to swallow. We have an arrangement with the oxygen people. Wyatt and K call every day. Joseph and Everest make midday runs, to make sure that we're okay.

"Hanging on," I tell them.

"You're doing fine," they say.

Fine is not okay.

Harvey is sad, because cats get sad. He sits by the door. He is waiting.

November has come in. November and rain. November and mist. November and Thanksgiving, and when Thanksgiving comes the Muni comes to us—Wyatt and K and Joseph and Everest and Sam in a pickup and a Harley. They set up in Grandma

Aubrey's room with a checkered cloth upon her bed. They slice the turkey and scoop the squash and potatoes and Wyatt's homemade gravy and the blueberry pie that Wyatt baked with the berries that she'd frozen.

"Oh my," Grandma Aubrey said. "Now this is living."

The news on the hopper is that all eight prospects turned up empty, all the leads are dead-end leads, the TV channels have lost interest, the feature writers have found other features. The hospital committee that took the hopper on as its celebrity charity won't keep her on much longer. In a few more weeks her therapy will be done, and she'll be discharged, and still nobody is saying, at least to us kids, where she will go. There's a new lady named Marie from a place they call the Young Center who has been spending time lately at the hospital talking to the hopper, coordinating with social services, answering questions, standing by, taking more and more charge of the situation. "This is good news," Nurse Cara had told us. "This is good help. Marie is giving her the space she needs; she's coming every day, she's waiting." "Waiting?" K asked. "Waiting," Nurse Cara said, "in case she decides to tell her story." Marie will keep ICE away, Nurse Cara said. Marie will keep her out of the hands of the Office of Refugee Resettlement. She will keep her from having to confess the names of people she loves, people that she seems to be protecting.

Marie will do everything she can, but still: there are so many questions.

Ana Celeste is a puzzle with a seam up one arm and a tilt in her walk and a folded bird where a secret lives, a name: Mauricio Flores. Ana Celeste is a pretty girl with hair running down past her shoulders.

Sometimes, on her day off, Nurse Cara comes to the house to visit us. Sometimes she'll do nurse things with Grandma Aubrey. Sometimes she'll tell me the truth, but she'll tell it kind. She likes the things that we have hung from Grandma Aubrey's ceiling. She likes the books on the book wall. Sometimes she sits reading out loud from something that once flew in through the Little Free Library in the blue valley. She turns the pages of *Earth*, and Grandma Aubrey whispers what is there, teaches her the magic.

*Phosphorescent moss.*

*Glacial lakes.*

*Clay fissures.*

*Volcanic plumes.*

Words K would like because of all the letters they use.

Words I wish I could show him.

"Sophie? Cara?"

"We're here. Right here. What is it?"

"Just checking."

And this is how it is, and the nights are long, and we wear our coats, we wear our blankets.

The wind blows through.

There are stars.

# THIRTY-FIVE

"SWEETHEART," NURSE CARA SAYS. "There's news."

Day's gone, night's in, it's wintertime dark. Nurse Cara stopped by after work to help Grandma Aubrey with the things Grandma Aubrey says a granddaughter shouldn't do. Bathroom things. Sponge bath things. Switch out the oxygen tank, clean the tubes things. Measure the blood pressure, count the pulse things. Grandma Aubrey is shrinking in the white sheets in the white bed.

Sometimes I think she's dreaming out loud. I don't know who she's talking to. I don't understand what she's saying. And then she comes back, and she is my Grandma Aubrey, and I read her the story of the Orbiter again. I read her stories about fog. I go back in time, to the blue valley and the *boing boing boing* of Sophie Blanchard inside our skies. And then she's hungry or she should be hungry, and I spread

Wyatt's jam-a-lade on a couple of crackers, and Grandma Aubrey takes the smallest mouse bites of mouse bites.

"Delicious," she'll say. The whole word in one breath.

I've taken the pillow off of my bed. The sheets and the blankets. The little pink pig I have had since before I remember. I've set myself up for sleep beside my grandma's bed, just in case she needs something in the middle of the night. Something I can actually, factually do. There's hardly anything like that, but sometimes there is, and I am here, and I am ready to be ready for my grandma.

"What kind of news?" I ask Nurse Cara now.

"Ana Celeste," she says.

My heart jumps.

"She's all right?"

"She's all right."

"She's talking?"

"Not yet.

"So that's the news?" I ask. "She's still not talking?"

"The news," Nurse Cara says, "is Wyatt."

"Wyatt?"

We sit at the kitchen table with two hot-chocolate mugs and a box of Wheat Thins. She's let her blonde hair down out of its high ponytail. She wears a brown and yellow sweater over her mint green uniform, those gloves that don't have glove fingers. There are purple patches beneath both eyes. Her Tirednesses, she calls them, touching them whenever Grandma Aubrey says, "But dear, you . . . look . . . exhausted."

"What?"

"She wants to tell you herself."

"Okay," I say. "She can tell me. I try to remember the last time I saw Wyatt. Three days ago. Four. "Special delivery," she said, when she came in through the door. Two jars of jam-a-lade. The crackers.

"She's waiting at the Muni. She and K both. Hop in my Cooper. We'll drive."

"She could call here," I say, "and tell me."

"She could."

"She could stop by."

"But that's not what she wants. She wants to tell you at the Muni."

"But I can't," I say.

Nurse Cara stares at me under the bulb of light that doesn't have a shade.

"Can't leave Grandma Aubrey."

"She won't be alone. I'll be here. I'll find her a book. Read her a story."

"She'll be alone when you drive me."

"Not for long, Sophie. Besides, your grandma's insisting that you go. Don't make her fight you on this one. She doesn't have the energy."

I shake my head.

"You are a most excellent granddaughter."

I shake my head again.

"She wants you to be a kid. She wants to see you happy. Out with your friends. Out in the weather. It does her no good to worry about you. She wants to know that when she goes—"

"Don't talk about it—"

"That you'll be okay."

I shake my head another time. "Won't be."

Nurse Cara wraps both hands around her mug. She brings it to her lips. She sips. She gives me that allover look, and I try to imagine what she sees. A plain girl with tangled auburn hair. A girl with a short nose and thin, pale lips. A girl with eyes the color that sad is. A girl in a long red coat and a dark blue scarf who cannot look straight back over the table.

Because the kitchen light is so much blare. Because her grandmother is dying and life is full of puzzles.

"What do you want most, Sophie?" Nurse Cara says.

"I want Grandma Aubrey to live."

"What do you want second most?"

"To do something that will make her happy."

"Right," she says. "Exactly."

She swallows the rest of her hot chocolate in one long swallow. She goes down the hall and gets her coat. She checks in with Grandma Aubrey and then comes back to me.

"Come on," she says. "Your friends are waiting."

# THIRTY-SIX

"THERE," NURSE CARA POINTS, from the inside of her Mini Cooper. She's parked in the dirt, beside the tower.

I release my belt. Look up through the dashboard. See the observation window all lit up by candlelight, and Wyatt and K in the flicker of it, waving on their side of the window. The one side of Wyatt's hair has grown all the way in, and the other side has been cut shorter. K has his Sinatra hat on and one of Everest's old coats, its hem down to his ankles, which I can see because the window glass runs full floor to full ceiling.

"Joseph will bring you home when you're ready."

"But—"

"He already knows. We've discussed it."

"Tell Grandma Aubrey—"

"She'll be fine."

"If anything—"

"We know where to reach you."

I climb out of the car, shut the door behind me, and watch Nurse Cara drive the drive, away. When I look up again, K and Wyatt are still waving. There's cold in the breeze that blows and a whole sky full of stars.

Getting up means climbing.

I walk the weedy walk toward the metal ladder in the night that I can see through, thanks to the candlelit room up above. The metal rails are cold; they're hard. The old paint peels away into my hands, and I should have brought my gloves. I pull and climb, and I'm higher. I pull and I climb, and the ladder wraps the tower, around and around in a spiral, and every time I make it around again, I stop to catch my breath—look out or look up or think of Grandma Aubrey, waiting alone until Nurse Cara gets back.

I feel K and Wyatt above me. I see the flicker of their lit wicks on the grass below, and I'm almost there, ready for the hopper news. Ana Celeste, stronger now and ready to leave and needing a place to go home to, needing to trust Marie, because Marie is someone to be trusted. I'm catching my breath and looking down and away at the tarmac and the Muni to one side and the field and the forest to the other, and it's cold out here on the ladder. The ladder spirals four stories tall. It's not so far now—the platform and the door with the rusty lock that was busted open years ago and stayed busted, because nobody comes here, not anymore. Just us, when we are looking for a hideout. Just us, here, when the hopper fell. When we stood here and watched and went running.

Whatever news there is hides in this tower. My friends are waiting. My grandma's dying.

My blue boots squeak and squeal into the sky. There's the smell of Wyatt's latest bake steaming through the busted-lock door and also the smell of the candle wax, and I'm that much closer, and now I see Wyatt and K on the platform above me.

"You made it," Wyatt says. She puts out her hand. She helps me the rest of the way up. She pulls me inside. K helps.

The shivery light.

The candles.

"Hey."

"Hey."

"Hey."

High fives, and I'm out of breath. I stand there breathing all the white smoke of the cold from my lungs. I stand there looking at Wyatt and looking at K, the color of his eyes, which are the color I remembered. You can't forget K's eyes. I know that now, standing here, no matter what is next, no matter how old I'll get. I will never forget those eyes.

Now: the old desk. The chair on its wheels. The bones of a bird on a sill. The clay pots with the plants died back down to the dirt. The globe, the books, the thick dust on the window glass, the dead tree in a basket, the bare twiggy limbs of the tree dressed up with faded Mardi Gras beads. The sculpture built of paper clips. The pen tossed into the empty drawer of a desk.

The room with a view, we call it.

"Thought you weren't going to come," K says.

"I came," I say, still breathing hard. "Didn't I?"

"We've been waiting close to an hour."

"Longer than that," Wyatt says.

"You could have just called, if it was so urgent important."

"Nope."

"Or come over."

She shakes her head.

We call this place ours even if we're hardly here. We've dragged our hands through its dust. We've pretended to tell the stories of the men we think might have worked here once, tracking the radar and the planes, talking the control tower talk. Wyatt cuts across the room and sits at the desk, and I see it now, all spread out—the aerial map and the red circles.

She makes a note. Pulls at her ear.

"It's been a puzzle," she says now.

"What has?" I ask.

"Why every one of our prospects turned up short. Why we couldn't find any proof of the hopper."

"Ana Celeste."

"Yeah. Everest went up in the Cessna with Sam, and then he went up with Joseph. None of them saw anything. They touched down empty-handed."

"Then?" I ask.

"And then—" K says.

"Then we studied the map again," Wyatt says. "We tried to figure out what we were missing. What we had not seen."

"We started over," K says.

"Looked at every possible locale. Thought it

through again. A hopper needs equipment. Equipment needs space. A hopper needs ground to take off from and ground to touch back down and a fan to fill the balloon with air."

"I know" I say.

"So—"

"What?—" I say.

"All these barns. All these abandoned places. All these open spaces. It's like—half of Gilbertine."

"Maybe not half," K says.

"Close enough."

Wyatt stands and grabs a cupcake from the tin she brought up here, carried it sideways, I guess, in her backpack. She grabs a cupcake for me and a cupcake for K, and my hands are still cold, but I pull away the wrapper off and taste the warmth of it.

"Good," I say. "So good." You could never ever stay annoyed with Wyatt. Her goodness is there, in every baked thing she bakes.

"Cupcakes are a Twenty Four fave," Wyatt says, and shrugs like she doesn't understand how that is, given how simple cupcakes are. She finishes hers and wipes the crumbs from her mouth. "We found," she says, going back to the map, "this one more possible place. Big enough. Abandoned enough. Worth doing surveillance on."

She pokes her finger at the map. The candlelight flickers.

"Okay."

"So Everest and Joseph went back up in the plane. And guess what they saw?"

I don't guess because who needs to guess. I'm here, after all. Waiting on the news they have.

"Enough to make them think that this could be the place."

She shows me the place on the map that's been circled in blue. Pulls the map closer to the candlelight, then K picks up another candle and touches more light to the spot. She points to somewhere close to the edge of town. Right there, on the Gilbertine border.

"Her story is out there," Wyatt says, pointing through the window. "Where she came from. What she's lost. If we find it we will understand. If we understand we can tell her that. Maybe that's all we can do—is understand. Maybe we're finally close to that."

The candlelight makes the room look wobbly. It draws the deep and the serious into Wyatt's forehead.

"This could be it," she says, and now it's her voice that wobbles, and now she crosses the room to find the ring of keys that are hung from a nail on the wall. She jiggles open the second lock and opens up the second door, which leads to the tower balcony, which runs three-quarters of the way around.

She steps outside.

We follow.

We are high in the air. We walk the balcony. If we reach, maybe, we'll touch the stars and the moon, which is a quarter moon, a broken moon, and still beautiful. Out there, beyond us, is Gilbertine—the pinwheels and the goats and the houses and the roads and all the land and all the farms and the Twenty Four and the steepletops and Grandma Aubrey and Nurse Cara in the cottage. Closer in is the runway, the Muni, the humps of the roofs of the huts, the smoke that could still be rising from Wyatt's factory, but it's too dark for us to see it.

The atmosphere curls. K leans in, looks up. The wind blows the one side of Wyatt's hair to the other side, and it's perfect up here and perfectly cold, and still I feel like I don't know why Wyatt couldn't tell me all the news by phone, why she insisted that I leave my Grandma Aubrey. There are so many stories, and some of them end, and some are just beginning.

Wyatt stands with her back against the tower window. I stand beside K, near the warmth of K, and we just stand there like that until Wyatt says:

"Hundreds of miles and fifteen years."

And I have no idea what she means by that.

And I know not to ask her.

I stuff my hands into my coat pockets. Tuck my chin into my coat.

She closes her eyes. She lifts her hands to brush her hair. When K moves, I hear a jostle in his jacket pocket, and now I see that he's stolen two strands of the Mardi Gras beads from the dead tree behind us.

One for me and one for Wyatt.

She takes the strand.

She fits her hand inside her pocket.

She holds, in it, the rattle.

Now she clicks the strand through her fingers like she's counting and doesn't shake the rattle.

Don't ask.

Wait.

Shhh.

"Hundreds of miles," she says again, "and fifteen years." The moon is only a quarter of itself, and I'm not breathing. I'm not stopping whatever's coming next.

"I come from a family called Singer," Wyatt says. "My father was a pilot. All the time, he wanted to know, *Where are we going this weekend?* Every single weekend he said it. *Let's go. Flying. Where?*

"Your father was a pilot?" K asks. "Your first father?"

I shake my head in the cold night air.

"Don't," I say. "Let her tell it."

Wyatt clicks through the beads. Her fingertips are blue. I can see that in the candlelight glow. I can see it because it is true.

"We were the Singers of Miami," Wyatt says. "We were always, like I said, flying. One weekend my dad decided on Gilbertine. He wanted to see it. So on that weekend, there we were. Up in the air. Headed north. For the joy of it."

Wyatt's mother is second-in-command of the plane, Wyatt says. Wyatt is first-in-command of Baby Winston, who is strapped into the seat beside Wyatt and is banging his fists together like a pair of cymbals from the first second the plane rambles down the Miami runway and rises. "Oh my God," she says, "he's crying. He's arching his back, hollering hard, five teeth in his mouth, hollering, and we're flying, and we're flying. It's a racket."

The plane is above the clouds, sometimes inside the clouds, Wyatt says, and Winston is crying. Sound like you've never heard, Wyatt says. Sound that will not stop. Hours and miles until Wyatt is saying, "We're almost there, Winston. We're almost coming in for a landing."

She can see it herself, she says, through the plane windows. The green land and red barns and generous air of Gilbertine. The rounded roofs of the Quonset huts. The black scratch of the tarmac.

Wyatt fits her finger into Winston's fist. She tells him to look out now, *See how the plane is lowering now, see how close we are getting to the ground, see there, Baby Winston, there are the trees, the green green trees and the silver creeks and the banks of grass, the white fence like a cowgirl fence, the big blue house where the planes are sleeping, the black flat of the runway—Almost there, Winston. See?*

*Get him to shhhh,* Wyatt's mother is saying,

Wyatt says. *Get him to shhhh. Wyatt. Please. Your fa-*
*ther needs his concentration. Plane is landing.*

But Winston won't shhh. He's filling the plane
with his unhappy howl, too much of it now, *Stop it,*
*Winston.* Wyatt's father thinks Wyatt isn't trying
hard enough. Wyatt's father is asking Wyatt: You
touching his toes, Wyatt? *You touching that feath-*
*er spot on the top of his head? You sing to him now.*
*Almost there. Tell him.*

Wyatt says.

Out here in the cold night, Wyatt is saying.
Clicking through the Mardi Gras beads, holding that
rattle. Catching the starlight in her eyes while the
candles burn in the room behind us, and the hopper is almost well, and so she'll vanish soon, and
Grandma Aubrey is down, down, down the road,
maybe sleeping, maybe having just a spoonful of applesauce, maybe brushing her hand against Harvey's
whiskers, saying to Nurse Cara, *Good for her, out*
*with her friends.*

Something?

And now Wyatt is singing. The fly-a-kite song.
With tuppence for paper, your own set of wings song,
through the atmosphere, she is singing. She is patting

her brother's head and rubbing his toes and making funny cross-eyed faces, but she can't make Winston stop crying. She is singing but Winston won't stop, until finally Wyatt's mother is saying, *Give him to me now. Let me have him.*

And Wyatt lifts her brother up.

And he screams a little louder.

And her mother reaches.

And the baby kicks.

And everything turns.

And everything swerves.

Because everything will.

Wyatt clicks through the beads. She stops, but then she starts again about the girl named Wyatt and the baby boy who bucks and pounds his fists. And shakes his head no. And arches up. And just a minute before all of this happens, Wyatt is holding Winston to the window saying, *Look, almost there,* but they aren't almost there enough, and Wyatt's brother won't stop.

Wyatt leans forward. Her mother turns back. Puts her arms out for the baby boy who kicks his feet and pounds his fists. Winston is peeling away, and Wyatt's mother almost has him, over the seat, through the wedge of open air in that Piper Twin,

Winston flailing against his airplane ears and the machinery, and that's when it happens, when the whole world flips.

"Flips?" K says.

Don't, I say with my eyes. Don't stop her.

But she stops. It's so many blinks of starlight before she starts again.

"The world was upside down," she says.

*Crash positions*, Wyatt's father says. Said. *Mayday Mayday Mayday*, and all Wyatt can hear is the howling like an animal of the engines, the crash of trees and plane, the shattering of wings and her brother not crying, her mother not talking, her father.

*Shhhh.*

Wyatt says.

All the bones and blood of her body in her ears, she says.

The trickle of a creek.

The hiss like a match just got to burning.

A squirrel's four feet on the flipped-over belly of the plane.

"The plane is an egg that is cracked," Wyatt says.

The blades of one propeller still spin, chew through the new flesh of a forest rhododendron. Fire eats into the trees and into the flesh above the popped bone of Wyatt's wrist, and there is the creek, the cold on her bare feet, the terrible sizzle, and Winston has stopped crying.

The woods, Wyatt says, are hard thorns and tall birch and sweet pine. The woods break at the far-off edge of themselves into light, and Wyatt feels the squirrel watching, sees a fox out in the shadows, hears the sound of her bare feet running, the splinters of her feet are running—through the burr and thorns and shadows into light, across the bank of grass, toward the little house.

*With your feet on the ground, you're a bird in flight.*

And now, in the control tower, Wyatt stops. She looks down and away toward the house of Joseph Bell and says, "He'd heard us. He was running."

Joseph Bell. With his white hair and his blue eyes and his ears so small on his head and his house with just himself inside and his factory, which wasn't a factory yet, which was just a shed, which was empty. Was running.

Everybody's story is the start of another person's story. And also, sometimes, the end.

Wyatt looks from K to me and me to K. The breeze snags the folds of his coat, and the clouds are white ink against the dark sky. And the stars are freckles.

"You ever wonder if the people who are gone can see us?" Wyatt asks, her eyes closed. "My mom and dad and Winston? K's mom? Your mom? Your Grandma Aubrey's Sophie Blanchard? People can't just vanish, can they? People are too alive for that."

"I wonder," K says, and he takes my hand and squeezes.

"Yeah," I say. I squeeze back.

"Winston had two teeth on the top and three on the bottom," Wyatt says. "My mother wore a braid to one side. I can't remember which side."

"My mother," K says, "was beautiful. I remember that."

I don't say anything about my mother.

"The hopper's story," Wyatt says. "Maybe it hasn't vanished yet. Maybe there's still time for us to find it."

The quarter moon is the color of milk. It's so cold out here that if I touched my nose that part of my nose would fall off. Our breath is smoke that's rising. Some of the candles inside are starting to wick out. There is less and less light and more dark out here, but not inside our hearts.

"We're going to the place tomorrow," Wyatt says, "where we think the hopper hopped from. Joseph and Everest and K and me—just us for now, just us and you. We're hoping you can come."

Another secret.

"But tomorrow's Tuesday."

"Taking the day off."

"But Grandma Aubrey—"

"She wants you to come. Just ask her."

"Yeah?"

"Ask her. I already did."

"Wyatt," I say, because none of us are moving, because I can't. Because suddenly I know something that I didn't know before, the answer to a question I had forgotten I should ask.

"Yeah?"

"The rattle."

"Yeah. It belonged to Baby Winston. You found the past I thought I'd lost. You found the story so that I could tell it."

There are so many kinds of love. Sad and gone and high and short. Deep and blue and red.

# THIRTY-SEVEN

THE ROAD ISN'T WIDE, isn't straight. Everest drives with both hands on the wheel, his shoulders up, and Joseph sits beside him. Wyatt and K and me sit three across in the back, K in the middle between us, his hand touching my hand, his shoulder rubbing my shoulder. Old tin cans roll around on the floor at our feet, a stack of newspapers piled high on one side, a couple of empty wire hangers, maps, an oil can with the word SUNOCO.

There is more land between the houses than there was a few miles back. There are kids chucking a ball against the side of a house and plaid sheets frozen on a line. Then nothing. Then a couple of old cars rattling toward us and dogs off their leashes, and now a deer shows up on the side of the road, its antlers heavy on its head.

Snow will come soon, I think. The sky is snow colored.

The road is breaking up. The road turns to gravel. The stones ping up against the belly of the truck. The road forks, and there's a house here and a house there and no houses and now a gas station with a convenience store and one kid hanging outside, bored and smoking. Then a fox shows up and then nothing, and now Everest puts his foot on the brake. He slows things down.

"That's it," Joseph says, pointing, and we look. A long drive of pebbles, and at the end of that, a barn.

Everest turns.

Cuts the truck to almost no speed, and we hardly breathe, crushing the rocks and shortening up the distance.

"You keep your eyes out for ... anything," Grandma Aubrey had said, when I was leaving, early this day, giving her a kiss on the cheek and pulling the blankets up to her chin. "You keep your heart ... on compassion."

I thought of the look on Wyatt's face last night, beneath the stars and quarter moon, a rattle tangled up inside the beads that she'd been counting.

*No no no no no,* she said. Then *yes.*

*Yes.*

The night was so cold.

The candlelight was dying.

"Would never have been found," I said, after a long time, "without the hopper," and Wyatt's tears were like diamonds fallen down from the sky, and K saw it, I know that K did. The whole length and glow of Wyatt. Her history just starting. An answer to the question we were never going to ask her—just follow Wyatt, just taste her blues, just climb the tower— Wyatt taking charge of things down here because up there in the sky she had no say at all, she had no choosing she could make, she could not stop the terrible of the terrible that was happening.

An upside-down plane.

A fire in the trees.

A hole in the woods and the heart.

A little girl running.

Out of the forest and then back into the forest when the hopper came down in a storm.

Rescue operation.

We ride together, side by side, the bump of the rattle in the pocket of the coat Wyatt is wearing and the rattle making rattle sounds when the truck shakes side to side and the truck crawling on, closer and closer, past trash cans without their hats, past a wagon without its wheels, past the long snake of an old rubber hose, past a rusted sewing machine, just sitting there in the cold of the weather, and now we're there, at the end of the drive, and the barn ahead is big. It's massive.

Whitewash on low stones. Broken slats for faded siding. Big old rooster up on the roof—a banged-up weather vane. The wheels of the truck send up dust, and the closer we get the better I see that there is no proper front door to the place, just something hanging off its hinges. The windows are high, and they're half broken too, and there are places where the smashed glass looks stitched together with the yarn of spiderwebs.

Everest stops, still at a distance. Puts the car into park. Shuts down the engine.

"The kids should wait here," Joseph says, turning to look back at us like he's seeing us on this day for the first time—the misfits of the Muni. His ears are red with the cold. The muscles in his neck are thick with strain. I picture him running now, through the forest, after Wyatt's plane went down—the fire and the smoke and the crash and the girl coming his way, and that was it, the day when everything changed. When a girl came to live at the house of Joseph Bell, with the men of 'Nam—a girl who'd turn a shed into a blues factory and an old man into a father.

"We're all in on all this," Wyatt says, the first thing she's said this entire drive. "Together."

"She's right, Joseph," Everest says, opening his door, stepping out, not slamming it behind him.

Joseph nods. "All right," he says. "Okay. But Everest and I take the lead."

"Ten-four," Wyatt says, and we nod.

We all pile out.

We walk the crunch of the drive with as much quiet we have in us.

The hinges creak.

The air inside is cool and damp.

The snow-colored sky blows in behind us.

Have you ever seen a museum of leftover things?

Have you ever seen anything like what it is that we see?

A world built out of the broken. A world nobody knows is here. Except for the people who have lived here. How many people?

"Some kind of squatting situation," Joseph says.

"I'll say," Everest says.

If you could run across the place it'd take you a long couple of minutes. You couldn't run across the place. It's piled high with stuff.

"Will you look at this?" K says.

A pad of origami paper.

Wyatt shakes her head. Will not believe.

The cold air comes out of our lungs when we breathe.

# THIRTY-EIGHT

THROUGH THE CRACKS in the concrete floor grow hairy weeds. In the pots on the sills of the windows the plants are dead. From the splinters of the rafters above our heads sheets have been hung—two sheets pinned together, three, and none of the sheets the same color. The sheets fall from the rafters to the floor. They cut the bigness of the place into rooms, but the walls of the rooms flutter in and out with the breeze. The walls do not stay in one place.

K closes the door, but there's no closing that door, not with the busted hinges. Everest and Joseph stand looking one way and then the other, and then Everest goes to the darker parts of the barn, and Joseph goes toward the lightest, and we three kids stick together.

We hear the shuffle of our boots. We hear the scuffle of something far away—a squirrel on the roof or maybe a mouse in the walls, I think, and when

I look up into the rafters I see the mourning dove. Two doves. They bob their heads. They spread their wings. We walk quietly, but our boots still talk, and now the doves fly, and a feather falls loose and comes spiraling down, lands at K's feet.

We walk. Our boots talk. We hear the echo of Everest and Joseph, but we cannot see them except when the wind runs through the sheets.

"Whoa," Wyatt says, and we walk, and here is a rowboat named TANGO, its prow painted a new bright red. Here is a bike built for two, streamers hanging from its handlebars. Here is the long U of a mini railroad track set up on empty boxes, with a mini train waiting to run, and from the rafters hangs a model Red Baron plane, its propeller painted yellow, and here is a box of toy cars with a shine to them and a box of old shoes with new laces and an antique cradle, and inside the cradle is a doll in rhinestone shoes.

A green couch, a red chair, two cots. And between the cots a woodburning stove, and an old TV, its rabbit ears propped up with a rifle. A silver pole hangs horizontal from a pair of chains, and from the pole hang a pair of white shirts and a polka-dotted sweater and some trousers, and now the wind blows in behind us, and the sheet-walls ripple, and there's the smell of varnish, paint, metal tools, and something rotting. Wyatt pulls a pale-striped sheet to one side, and we see what she sees—a table and two chairs, an almost empty jar of peanut butter and a knife, the brown pulpy flesh of two Granny Smiths, boxes and boxes of Cracker Jack, crackers, and barrels and barrels of apples.

"Whoa," she says again. "Man."

In the nowhere of here someone lives, or lived, turning broken things into brand-new things, junk stuff into rescued stuff, like a Santa's workshop in one of those books when the future has come and the planet is ending. It's been more than three months since the last flight of the hopper. Whoever lives here provisioned up, as K might say. Whoever lives here lived off the grid, and then some.

"Everest?" We hear Joseph now. "Kids?"

We follow his voice. We push through the sheets. Empty boxes of crackers and empty cartons and copper-bottom pans and more dresses and coats hung from hooks and the mourning doves above us and wires dangling near wires, the buckets of paint, the buckets of varnish, the brushes, a bucket of tools, a lamp with half a plastic globe for a shade, an old sewing machine, a pincushion. When we find Joseph he's standing by another off-hinge door where, looping loose from rusting hooks and hangers are cables and tethers. A crashed-out bench sits up against the wall. A pair of propane tanks. An inflator fan and a generator. Books on the floor, a map pinned to the wall, math on paper.

Everest leans over. Digs through things. Stands back up with a book in his hand.

"Somebody came up here and took over," he says. "Place must have been abandoned. Whoever found it knew what they were doing."

"Ingenious tinkerer," Joseph says.

"Straight down to diverting the electricity," he says, pointing to the wires overhead, then down across the floor, then outside across the open land and down and to wherever the power is that somebody else must be paying for. "Instructions for flying," he says now, looking at the book in his hand, a picture of a hopper on the cover. He thumbs through, and it's easy to see the color pictures and the diagrams, the math somebody wrote in the margins.

"Like one of Grandma Aubrey's stories," I say.

"Who does this?" Everest says. "Who can?"

"The hopper," Wyatt says. "Our hopper."

"Not alone, she didn't," Joseph says. "Nobody does all of this alone."

I think of the clean girl in the clean bed and all her broken parts. I think of the parts of things that fell from the sky—the balloon with its patches, the bench with its splinters, the pink patent leathers, and the man who paid with crumpled cash. Whoever else was here never came for her. *Mauricio Flores*.

Ana Celeste is a genius.

"So she built a balloon," K says.

"Or she found one here and fixed it up," Joseph says. "Or someone did."

"And she taught herself to hop," K says.

"Or someone helped her," Everest says.

"That makes two," Wyatt says.

"Two geniuses," I say.

"At the very least," Joseph says. "Two of them in an abandoned barn. Fixing what they found."

Living, I think, and I think how all the words in the world will not be enough words to tell it true to Grandma Aubrey. I will tell it a thousand times and a thousand ways, but that won't help her see it. This is a see-it-with-your-own-two-eyes world. This cannot be believed.

"She went hopping in a storm," Wyatt says, trying to put it all together. "She went out into the wind on purpose. There must be a why for that."

"Maybe we'll never know," Everest says. "Some things you can't."

"We should take her something," I say, "to show her that we've been here. That we understand."

"Yeah," Joseph says. "We can do that."

"They said . . ."

"Doesn't matter. What's right is right. We'll do it."

He touches the door with his boot. It creaks open even wider to the stretch of long, brown grass, the snake of wires, a shed. Plenty of room to hop from and to land, I think. Plenty of sky to float into. He steps out, and we step out. We look out over the farms and the air of Gilbertine. Feel the wind in the tunnel of our throats.

There's the trickle of a creek just beyond.

There's a pileup of buckets. More brushes. More tools.

There's a shed.

"Outhouse," Joseph says.

"Not in my whole life," Everest says, "could I have imagined this. Not even in 'Nam would I have seen it."

"Almost everything," Joseph says, "we still don't know."

"That inflator fan," Everest says now, and Joseph nods.

"I know."

"Someone brought it back inside after the accident. Somebody had to. Someone was here when she hopped. Someone knows she didn't come home."

"Let her go off in the storm," K says.

"Let her go and not go searching for her," Wyatt says.

"They thought she was dead," I say. "Has to be that."

"All the news," Wyatt says. "All the headlines. Couldn't be that."

"I don't know," I say. "Had to be something."

Inside the barn, the mourning doves mourn. Out here the cold wind blows, and the creek trickles, and there's frost on the buckets and the brushes. Through the bare trees we can see parts of Gilbertine.

Grandma Aubrey's waiting. Nurse Cara. We should go back.

I'm the first to turn.

Wyatt's the first to gasp.

There's a girl at the door with the busted hinges.

Her long dark curls fall halfway to her waist. Her puffy coat is a thousand ways too big. Her feet are filthy dirty inside sandals.

"Hello," I say.

"Hello."

"Hello."

In our quietest voices. In our shock.

"Marisol?" she says. "Marisol?" She cries.

The girl can't be more than eight or nine. The girl looks like the hopper. If we move too fast, she'll run.

"Shhh," I say. "Shhh." Taking one step and the next step, Wyatt just behind me, K following, and the girl's eyes are so big, the fringe of her lashes are so long, her coat is so big, her feet are dirty, her feet—they have to be freezing.

"We're her friends," Wyatt tells the girl. "Ana Celeste. Her friends." She points to herself. She points to all of us. Trying to turn English into Spanish.

# THIRTY-NINE

THE GIRL RIDES IN THE FRONT between Everest and Joseph. Back in the back are K, Wyatt, and me. We see the top of her head, the bubble of her curls, the blanket we pulled from the leftover things to wrap around her giant parka. She was shivering when we took her. She kept crying.

"Shhh," we said. "Shhh."

The same in English as in Spanish.

We can't see the doll with the rhinestone shoes on the girl's lap. Not from where we're sitting, in the cab, in the back.

The roads go from broken stones to asphalt to something wider. The spaces between the farms and houses are closer and closer than they were, until we're on the main road now, just passing the Twenty Four, Everest speeding past the clop of the horse-drawn carriage, past the girl on roller skates, past the Harleys even, and we're almost there, at the Muni, driving the drive to Joseph's house. I reach for Wyatt's hand, and she reaches for Winston's rattle. K tips forward in the cab like that could help Everest's truck get down the roads even faster. Now Everest jumps out before the engine's cut. He opens his door and hurries down the hall and gets the hot water in the bathtub running, and we're coming, we're coming, like we said we would when we were making plans, when Everest was driving.

"We'll get her a bath and into something clean. We'll get her a meal. We'll wait on calling the police. We'll wait. We can't do anything to scare her."

I say. Wyatt says. All of us agree.

Now Joseph is carrying the girl into the house, swooping her up into his arms, the blanket dragging behind them, the doll still in her hands. He's in through the door ahead of us, and we're right after that, Wyatt first, then me, then K. We can hear the water filling the tub and Joseph talking, quiet, quiet, to the girl still in the cradle of his arms, pressed against his beat-up jacket.

"Here," he says, about the doll she holds hard. "Let me take that."

But she holds on hard, and then she gives up. He props the doll up on the sink, where she can see it.

"She's yours," Joseph says. "She's not going anywhere."

Joseph is the one who has done this before. Joseph is the one who knew what to do once and knows what to do now, who holds the girl while Everest finds the fresh towels, the new soap, and slowly, slowly Joseph unwinds the blanket, unzips the parka, lowers the girl to the bathroom tiles, and then stands up and looks down at us, because we're all four behind him now, in the bathroom that is steaming up.

"Wyatt and Sophie," he says, backing away, giving the rest of the job to us. "Nice and slow. And gentle. You'd be scared too."

*You were scared*, he almost says to Wyatt.

The girl is huge eyed, but she's stopped crying. She is tiny underneath her parka, her too-big shirt, her pants that are too short, too tight, even for her tininess. She stands on the nubby bathroom rug while we finish peeling her clothes away, carefully we do it, Wyatt getting up to pour blueberry soap into the tub and then kneeling again beside me on the floor, and we both say, *Shhh*, and we both work gently, and we both know that if we move too quick we could get the girl scared again, crying, and how has she ever been out there alone in a big barn of broken things, alone, without the hopper? Stealing from where? Living like how? The convenience store at the gas station? Maybe. The convenience store with its peanut butter and its bread and milk, but that is only maybe.

Shhh, we say. We're your friends, we say. We will take you to the hopper.

She watches us.

She shivers.

*Marisol?*

We help her into the tub. We slide her in to the blueberry bubbles.

"I like blueberries," Wyatt tells her. "I just do."

Saying it like the girl understands, and maybe she does.

"I have a farm," Wyatt says. "Out there." She points. She draws rows of bushes into the steaming air with her hand.

"She's a baker," I say. "Wyatt is." I point to Wyatt. "Sophie," I say. I point to me. "Everest," I say. "Joseph. K."

*Trust us.*

*Hearts on compassion.* I think of Grandma Aubrey in her bed. I think of how glad she'll be, how glad when we tell her this story even if words won't be enough, even if nothing ever is.

The girl's dark curls spread out from her neck into the suds of the tub. The bubbles turn gray, then darker than that. We give the girl a cloth, and she lets the cloth float, and we can't even think how long it must have been since she sat in a bathtub at all. Wyatt takes Winston's rattle from her coat. She hands it to the girl. The girl won't take it, and then she does, and her hand disappears beneath the dirty bubbles.

"You stay with her," Wyatt says. "I'll get things ready."

She stands. She leaves the steaming room that smells like blues.

"Shhh," I say to the girl, who watches Wyatt leave and then looks, in a panic, for her doll. The doll's still there on the sink where Joseph left it. "You'll be all right. See?"

She looks at me with the hugeness of her eyes. Raises her hand and the rattle that's inside it. Plays the sizzle of old rattle music until her hand disappears again into the suds.

"You must have been scared," I say, "out there alone."

She doesn't say yes. She doesn't say no. She doesn't have to, and English is not her language. I wish that Spanish were mine.

"You must have been cold," I say. "You must have been lonely."

She watches what I say, but I don't know if she understands it.

I draw a picture of a balloon in the air between us. I draw a picture of a girl. "She fell but she's all right. We got her to a hospital. Pretty soon she'll be walking on her own two feet without any help at all from Mike. Or Nurse Cara."

Names the little girl can't know.

Words I can't draw with my hands.

The girl's not sure. Her eyes are huge. I don't tell her that the hopper won't talk or that she's been on the news or inside a flyer or that the people of Gilbertine did a GoFundMe fund or that the hospital let her stay, for the purpose of therapy, for the purpose of keeping her safe because no one came for her. The hospital let her stay, or maybe, like one rumor went, somebody rich paid her hospital bills, out of pocket, anonymous. There are things nobody has told us kids. There are things we don't understand. There are things we could never explain, but we've seen the hopper, and she's been eating Wyatt's blues. *Heart on compassion*, Grandma Aubrey said, and maybe that means to keep it simple right now, when too many words is just too many words, and very slow now, very delicate, I take a washcloth to her face and scrub away the dirt, like erasing the math off of Grandma Aubrey's chalkboard.

"We're her friends," I say. "We'll be your friends too."

I can hear Wyatt down the hall fixing up her room. I can hear Everest and Joseph talking to K, and now Everest's on the phone talking to Nurse Cara, and now I hear him talking to Grandma Aubrey, and now he's talking to Marie, repeating the story so that each of them can hear the news direct from the man who has it.

An abandoned barn at the edge of Gilbertine.

Some kind of squatter situation.

Creek water and an outhouse shed.

A convenience store.

A gas station.

Some things borrowed and some things stolen, and the genius of it, the outright genius.

Looks to be her sister.

"Yes," he says now. "We're thinking so. Hiding from something, that's for sure, but only the little girl, no other family on the premises."

"Yes," he says. "Sure."

He had looked. We had looked. We had pulled every wall built of sheets to the ground and flapped them out and looked into the shadows beneath the boat, beneath the cots, beneath the couches, and then outside again we'd gone, front and sides and back, but there was no one else there. Only this little girl and her peanut butter and rotten apples and proof of a cloud hopper.

"Yes," Everest says. "Of course."

"No, no, we haven't done that."

"Yes. We promise. We'll check with you first."

Wyatt's dragging big things in her room. She's banging something up onto her wall. Now she's down the hall and out the door, and now she's back inside again, her footsteps in the hall.

"We'll heat these," she tells Joseph, in the kitchen.

"All of it?" he asks.

"She's our guest," Wyatt says. "She's hungry."

Pans bang. The timer is set. "You think she's ready to come out now?" Wyatt says.

"I don't know," I say.

"You think we should just try?"

"I can try," I say, showing the girl what might happen next—how we'll lift her, dry her, get her dressed and warm and fed. A story I tell with my body and my hands until she pulls the rattle up out of the suds and then raises her other hand, and I think she means that it's okay, yes, I'll come with you. I trust you.

"Yes," I say. "She said yes."

We help her up. We drain the tub. We rinse the suds off with the shower head, and then we wrap the towels around her body and her head and carry her off to Wyatt's room where the smallest clothes that Wyatt owns are laid out on the bed. Three shirts, a skirt, a pair of pants, a dress, two sweaters, three pairs of socks in pink, yellow, and red, some underpants.

"You choose," Wyatt says.

The little girl drops the towel from her long wet hair, and maybe she understands.

"Pretty things," I say, and Wyatt says, "Don't rush her." Wyatt touches her own scar with her hand, and

I think again of the story that she told—of Wyatt crashing to the ground and running from the shatter—away from the plane, away from her mom, away from her dad, away from Baby Winston over the *pop pop pop* toward Joseph. Everything gone. Everything strange and a stranger, and we are strange, and we are strangers, and Wyatt says, "Let her decide. Give her time."

Because right here, for absolute sure, Wyatt knows best.

It's like the girl can understand, and maybe I want her to understand, to know everything I'm thinking without me saying what I'm thinking. On feet that look like they hurt when she walks, she walks toward the bed. She seems to like the green dress best. She picks it up, drops the towel, pulls it over her head.

Her wet hair making wet marks on the cloth.

Her feet still bare.

"Blues are warm," Everest says, from the kitchen.

"Coming," Wyatt says, but we don't move. We let the girl finish dressing like she wants to dress. We let her take her long look around Wyatt's room. The spoons and the books and the maps and the boots— she walks the room with the green dress to her ankles, her red socks on, like a Christmas present I think, and now when she stops at something, Wyatt gives her the word.

"Book," Wyatt says.

"Map," she says.

"Coat."

"Boots."

"Blueberry bush in a helmet."

The girl looks up to hear those words again.

"Blueberry bush in a helmet," Wyatt repeats, smiling this time when she says it. "Can't help it," she says. "I'm weird." She rolls her eyes to make fun of herself. Another Wyatt first. A bit of history.

The girl opens her mouth and laughs. It sounds like bubbles popping.

"Got your doll," K says, and he hands the girl the one thing that, right this second, is hers. She looks at him like I look at him, like she can see the magic.

She runs toward it, pulls it close.

She touches her hand to her belly.

"Look," Joseph says now, spreading a newspaper down on the floor where the little girl can see it. It's a picture of the hopper from a GoFundMe story. Sitting there, with both her casts, in her hospital bed.

"Marisol!" the little girl says. "Marisol!"

And she starts howling.

And that's how we know Marisol is the name of the hopper. And that Ana Celeste is the name of the girl.

"Shhh," we say. "Shhh. She's alive." K acts it out— the fall, the hospital bed, Nurse Cara.

"She's alive, she's okay," we tell the little girl. And we hope that she believes us.

# FORTY

NURSE CARA DID what we didn't think she could do, what anyone could do. Nurse Cara bought us time. Nurse Cara and Marie, who talked to the police who said yes, the hopper and the girl will be given that, no need to rush the intake, no need to take the two away, no need for immigration judges, asylum officers, police rules yet—no need for that right now. For now we're being hearts not rules. For now we're being family not strangers. For now Nurse Cara and Marie, and we should wait until tomorrow Nurse Cara said—to prepare the hopper, to prepare the little girl, to prepare ourselves, after all this time, for answers to the questions we couldn't ask because the hopper would not answer.

Now tomorrow's now, and all night long Grandma Aubrey and I have been awake in her room, the cold blowing in, the story I keep telling that I can't tell. No matter how many words I use.

"Living there," Grandma Aubrey keeps saying. "On . . . her own."

"Seems like."

"Heart—" she says, "breaking."

Joseph and Everest, they say ingenious. Never seen anything like it, they said. Never seen a place so broken down and so ready too, for anything. So much that was messed up. So much that was fixed. And so many barrels of apples. And crackers.

I've told Grandma Aubrey about the walls built from sheets. I've told her about the boat and the trains and the cars and the planes and the bikes and the wheels and the shoes and the inflator fan that was dragged back inside and also the cots and the woodburning stove, but the stove was cold, it hadn't burned wood in forever. I've told her about the doll and the blueberry bath and Wyatt laying her old clothes on her bed and how the girl's biggest word was the laugh that she laughed when Wyatt told her about the bush in the helmet. Then Grandma Aubrey said to tell it through again, because something's missing that she cannot figure out, something doesn't fit, a lot of things don't. There's too much coincidence and not enough too. Nothing like any of this should happen.

Two girls alone with their Spanish.

And one of them flying.

And a name we haven't worked out just yet. *Mauricio Flores*, inside a bird.

All we have is what I saw and the guessing that we put in between, and Grandma Aubrey doesn't fall asleep one time, and Harvey comes in for a nuzzle.

"Living there," Grandma Aubrey says, "in a barn full of someone else's things. Bikes. Planes. Trains. Wheels. Some kind of . . . transportation fiend."

"Guess so."

"My kind of people," Grandma Aubrey says.

"But Mauricio Flores," I say. "Must have been the man from the Doc Martens store. Must have been, right? Where is he?"

"That is the question."

"That is," I say, "more than one question."

Two girls is all we know for sure. Two girls, a barn of leftover fixed things, a hopper who figured out how to fix an old hopper and fly. "Never seen such a thing," Everest said. "Never seen it, even in 'Nam." Every good-weather day in the summer the hopper put on her show for us, and then here comes a bad-weather day that started out as a good-weather day, and she went out anyway with a bird and a question, and we don't know, and the clock ticks, and tomorrow's coming.

There'll be snow soon; there's that taste of a spoon in the air. There's skies and breeze and the moon rinsing in and out of the clouds like the clouds are a rolling sea, and our bones could hurt for the chill of it, but we have four blankets on and also the quilt that Nurse Cara made, something from her house that she brought with her.

"What would I do," she said, when Grandma Aubrey had protested, "if I had nobody to give my quilting to? I'd cut and stitch. For who?"

Cut and stitch, I think. The hopper can do that too.

In parts of Gilbertine Christmas is ready. The twinkle lights blinking on gutters, the holly on fence posts, the wreaths on doors, the fake candles in windows. At the Muni too they've been putting Christmas on, with a short little tree they cut out of the woods and topped with an aluminum-foil star. K made the star. He made the tinsel too. Then he made a paper chain that he hung from limb to limb.

Tomorrow or the next day, I think, I'll bring some Christmas here. I'll buy a Christmas tree and tinsel. I'll buy a light-up Santa at the hardware store and plug it by the kitchen window so the cows way out there can see. I'll buy jingle bells for the front door and a wreath for the bedroom door, and I'll buy Grandma a pair of thermal socks and a scarf for her neck, and I'll buy Harvey a new bowl and jeweled collar, and I don't know what else for who. I'll find the old radio we brought here from the valley and tune it to the Christmas songs, and I'll find the Christmas books in our wall of books and read them to my grandma.

I'll do that tomorrow, which is after today. Or I'll do that the day after.

Today we'll take the girl of the barn to the girl of the sky.

I cannot sleep.

It's still so dark.

# FORTY-ONE

SHE CARRIES THE DOLL with the rhinestone shoes, and she carries the doll from Wyatt's room. She wears the same green dress with a different sweater and a new pair of socks and a pair of old shoes that make her feet look like extra big feet on the tininess of her body. Wyatt has combed all the curls in the girl's hair and tucked them back into a ribbon, and all night long, Wyatt says, Wyatt slept beside her on the scratchy wood floor while the girl slept in Wyatt's bed beside the two dolls she won't let go of.

They drive down the road to pick me up, and when I open the door, Sam, the old 'Nam medic, is standing there with a takeout cup of the Twenty Four coffee in his hand and a box of emergency supplies. "Trading places," he says, and I'm as glad as anything that he'll be here for Grandma Aubrey when I'll be gone, glad for all the misfits of the Muni.

"That Wyatt?" Grandma Aubrey calls, her voice weak from a night of watching the window and listening to me imagine the story of the hopper, the story of the leftover things, the story of the little girl who will finally see her sister.

"That Wyatt coming in quick to see me?"

"It's Sam," I say.

"Oh, Sam," she says. "Sam. Thank you for coming."

Anything could happen.

Anything could happen anytime.

"Your heart on . . . compassion," Grandma Aubrey says now.

"I know."

"Stories take . . . time."

"Shhh, Grandma Aubrey," I say.

"You be," she says.

"Shhh."

I kiss both cheeks. I kiss them again. I look at Sam, already set up in the kitchen chair he carried here into the bedroom, his hat still on his head, his collar pulled up past his chin, Harvey on the floor by Sam's metal-toed boots thinking of taking a landing on a potbelly lap, thinking it, twitching his whiskers.

"I like a good stiff breeze," Sam says, when the wind blows in through the frosty open windows.

"Isn't it," Grandma Aubrey says, "something?"

"Reminds me," he says, "of a day in 'Nam."

"Oh," Grandma Aubrey says. "Tell me that story."

I step back and back toward the door.

I tiptoe down the hall.

I close the door behind me, climb into the back cab of the truck.

"Fast as we can," I say, and the little girl in the front lifts one of the dolls and waves back at me. The truck smells blue. Everest's driving.

# FORTY-TWO

I TRY TO THINK how we'd look from above—Everest and Joseph and Wyatt and K and me and the little girl and the two dolls. Out of the truck and across the lot and into the hospital and down the hall, past the lady with the owl glasses who waves us through, tugs at her skirt, stands up now—her body like a salute, her eyes on all those curls and that long green dress and those two too-big shoes.

*Hometown heroes* is what they should be. The little girl and also the hopper. Survivors, geniuses, ingenious tinkerers. Living on their own, invisibly.

*Undocumented immigrants* is what some people will say. People like the people from the headlines, from the TV. Where will they go? How will they be? How can we help?

We don't know.

What we know is that they're hardly different from the rest of us—all of us missing something.

Heart on compassion, like Grandma Aubrey says.

K carries Wyatt's latest bake, and I carry the doll from Wyatt's room, and Wyatt holds the hand of the girl, which doesn't carry the doll, and Everest and Joseph go up ahead, down the hall, toward the room where the hopper is dressed and waiting, where Nurse Cara is and Marie and Mike, just in case we need him or maybe because he wants to be here on this breakthrough day. It'll be a breakthrough day, the biggest breakthrough day, and he should be here.

Joseph saying to Everest, and Everest nodding in the truck, that our number one job is to give the two girls time together.

"Whatever we have to do," Joseph said. "The girls come first. Not the rules."

Everybody who knows us, because everybody knows us, waves as we pass by.

Wyatt leans down and kisses the girl on the head.

She says words that she hopes sound like Spanish.

"Soon," she says.

"Almost there," she says.

"You look so pretty," she says.

"Look," she says. "Your sister."

# FORTY-THREE

You ever seen a howl that isn't a howl of hurt but a howl of love, when the love hurts too? You ever seen two people hug so hard that you think their bones will shatter, the smoosh of a doll in between the hearts of the two of them, their curls all tangled?

The smoosh of two dolls?

You ever seen Wyatt crying like she is crying, she can't stop crying, the blues on the tips of her fingers rubbing the skin beneath her eyes, remembering, I'm sure she's remembering? Or two old 'Nam vets stepping away, outside this hospital conference room, into the hall, their eyes so full they cannot see you?

You ever seen K standing right beside you with his hat in one hand and his piece of sun in the other, turning it over and over, the weight of it, the sure thing of it too?

You ever seen when you can't see, because all the beauty's got you whipped? All the vertical miles of atmosphere where anything can happen and this does?

Some stories are stories that you don't know how to tell.

Some stories are stories better lived.

Some stories are now. Some are this. And still. Some stories are not yours to claim or keep. Some stories belong to nobody but two cousins who did everything they could to survive.

Because these two aren't sisters but cousins.

And Mauricio Flores is the name of the hopper's uncle.

And I can't tell you, because I don't know, what kind of genius it took for them to survive.

We know:

There will be more questions.

We know:

That we aren't the people who decide what happens next.

We know:

That we can't even guess what comes next.

We know:

That Marie can turn Spanish into English and English into Spanish, back and forth again.

*Si.*

Marisol talks.

She begins.

# FORTY-FOUR

"It was dark, so dark that I remember how the birds were sleeping. The doves. You see the doves? Always there. Our doves."

She starts like this. We wait.

Like this.

Marie: doing the translating.

"My uncle had been gone three days, and we could not find him. Three days of him missing. He had brought us from El Salvador. We came without our mothers."

Marisol stops.

She just stops.

Her eyes fill up, and Ana Celeste leans against her shoulder, listening to the story only Marisol will tell, Ana Celeste shaking her head whenever Marie asks her things in Spanish. Shaking her head, hugging the dolls on her lap, both of them now. Kicking her feet in her too-big shoes.

"My father," Marisol says, inside Marie's English. "They shot him dead in El Salvador. They were coming for our family. Our mothers said to go up north; it was all the money we had. They would come as soon as they could. We would send money back. Make a home. They'd come."

"Take your time," says Marie. She wears a white bun with three pens stuck into the knot of it. She sits in one chair, and Nurse Cara sits in the other, and the two girls sit, and the rest of us stand.

"I don't know all the names of all the places," Marie says, after Marisol says it first. "I don't know how long we lived in each. My uncle was a fruit picker. My uncle mowed lawns. My uncle washed dishes. My uncle fixed old cars. In the day he was gone, and at night he came back, and sometimes we worked with him when it was safe for us to work. When he heard about this place and the farms, we took a bus and then another bus, and he got work, and we found the barn. No people, just things, in the barn. Like somebody had lived there, and then someone had run, leaving everything behind."

Ana Celeste nods. She pulls the rhinestone shoes off of her doll and then snuggles them back on again.

She buries her face in the face of Wyatt's doll. She kicks her feet so hard I think her loose shoes might fall off. She lets Marisol do the talking. I'd thought the words had been knocked clear straight out of the hopper. I'd thought that no matter what she'd never talk again. I'd thought we could go out and find her story and give her back her story, but that's not how stories work. Stories belong to the people who live them. Stories are this, and we're listening.

"My uncle," Marisol continues, through Marie, "would leave in the morning in the dark and come home at night and stay up making the plane and the train and the boat into games for us. Big toys. Big somethings. In the morning he went back to work. He was saving for our mothers. So they could come."

She stops here, and that seems like it, all there is, all she will tell us. She whispers to Ana Celeste, and Ana Celeste whispers back, and Marie doesn't try to steal their secrets from Spanish into English. There's one rectangle of a window in this hospital conference room. Marisol stares into and past it now. She lifts her hand to her hair, and I see the long, long scar, like a sewing machine had needled up her arm.

K has been holding his chondrite all of this time. The rock that just looks like a rock unless you know its story. He leans toward Marisol and slips it into her hand.

"Yours," he says. "It'll help."

She turns it over. Looks at him.

"Tear of the sun," he says, and Marie translates. "Better than diamonds."

Marisol looks from the chondrite to K and back again. She shakes her head—yes, no—and then she starts again on her story.

"Aliens," Marie says when Marisol says it. "Illegals. These were their names for us. But the barn was ours. It was paradise."

*Paradise*, I think, and I think of how it was inside the barn on the hill out there where hardly anybody is. How the walls were sheets, and the air was cold, and the water ran in the creek below. And what was broken got itself fixed.

"Paradise," she says again, her Spanish into English. "Nobody there except for us, and every day was something new inside, something new to find, something new to fix, something new to us, and in the day my uncle worked, and in the day we passed the time, Ana Celeste and me in the barn with the things left behind. We found the big balloon when we were playing. We didn't know what it was."

Marie pulls a fresh pen out of her bun, shakes her head. She wants to ask a question. She does not. None of us want to get in the way of the story that belongs to the hopper and Ana Celeste and the man, wherever he is.

"He worked so hard on it," Marisol says. "He could do anything, and he could do this—make the balloon work, teach me to fly."

Ana Celeste shakes her head. Back and forth. Up and down.

Marisol turns the chondrite in her hand, and it's like Wyatt in the tower, clicking the beads and holding the rattle and talking back into time, the time we didn't know existed until Wyatt finally told us. I look at Wyatt now, standing beside me, the cross in her nose and the rings in her ears and the stain of the blues where the tears had been falling. I look at K, his hat smashed back on his head, and Joseph and Everest and Nurse Cara and Mike and Marisol and Ana Celeste and Marie, who is our bridge. Grandma Aubrey should be here, I think, Grandma Aubrey belongs with us. The mothers of these girls are gone and soon, I think, soon—

And then I won't think it.

I won't think of how Marisol felt in the hospital, two broken legs. How she felt, knowing Ana Celeste was out there. How she felt so unfree to do anything, to say anything, to confess anything. Because if she did, she'd have put her uncle and her cousin at risk.

You see it in the headlines.

You see it on TV.

She'd seen it everywhere she went.

There are no good choices when you are not free. When you live in a place invisibly.

"It isn't hard," she says. "To fly. It's just air and heat and strings and a balloon that needed fixing. You count your breath between the burns and go up and up then come back to where you started from. Early in the morning, before he left for work, my uncle showed me how to fly."

The perfect air, I think, of Gilbertine.

"That day," Marisol says through Marie, "started with sun. That day I was afraid, because my uncle was missing. He'd been gone three nights, and we were frightened. He had the money for our mothers now. He had it with him. He said he was taking it to the safe place and that after he'd gotten the money there he'd come back home. But he didn't come back, and I had to find him."

Ana Celeste starts crying now. Marisol holds her even tighter, her long arm across the shoulders of Wyatt's dress and Wyatt's sweater.

Where is the safe place? I think.

Mauricio Flores, I think. Gone.

"Take your time," Nurse Cara says now. Marie turns the words slowly into Spanish.

"He would have come back," Marisol says. "He would have never left us. I had to find him. I had to get up there and see if there was anyone down here who could help us."

"We were there," I say. "Watching you. Your pink Doc Martens."

"We were there every day," Wyatt says. "You were our show. Our spectacular."

"But the storm," K says. "It was coming. I felt it in my pinkie."

"*Si.*"

The storm was coming.

But first, she says, there was sun. First it was just

another summer day, and she got the hopper out, and Ana Celeste helped her with the inflator fan, and the burner burned, and she was off and she was up, watching the earth below, looking for her uncle, for the safe place where he was going. She was only looking for him, she says. She wasn't watching the weather like she'd been taught to watch the weather. There were more important things: her uncle was missing. She put his name in her pocket. In case something happened, and she fell down, she wanted somebody to tell him what had happened. She didn't know until it was too late that the atmosphere was jumbling. She didn't see how the mesh in garden fences started to curl. She didn't know until she looked over her shoulder that the sky was inking, the sky was bucking, an animal was coming.

It was like the sky was lots of skies, and they were running at each other, she says. The cold air under the warm air and the sun milking the horizon. Far away, she says, on the edge of everything she saw a ping of lightning. Like a needle pricking, she says, looking for the words. Like the sky putting on a show.

She was counting one two three. She was working the flame beneath the balloon to keep the balloon air hot, inflating. Then the rain came black. Then the hail, which was fists. Then the clouds were so thick it was like being in a blanket, and she could not see the up or the down of it. The birds were breaking. The trees were flying. The wind was waves. The clouds bucked.

The balloon went crazy.

Edge of the field, she says. Edge of the trees. The storm broke loose, and the hail was pounding. She was losing her heat. The balloon was wobbling. She dropped from the sky, and the earth came fast, and the last thing she remembers, she says, was the hard scrape of the trees and the balloon all the way popped and the smoke of the storm that was inside her now and the chirp of one bird singing.

And then the sound of you came running.

# FORTY-FIVE

WE DON'T ASK for any more.

We are hurt inside, our hearts our hurting. Our hearts are words we cannot say. English into Spanish, Spanish into English—it does not matter. Ana Celeste can't stop crying now. Marisol is crying too. She asks Marie if they can be, please, alone, please don't take us anywhere, please don't tell the cops who we really are, please don't let the cops go after Mauricio.

*Please.*

Marie promises them that they are safe. She tries to explain; I can hear her trying in Spanish. But the girls are still afraid, they are telling her things, they are telling Marie their own hard stories—showing with their hands the stories of people who got lost because they trusted. People who were driven away. People who now live in cages.

We leave them to each other in the hospital room. We leave them be for now. Two cousins who might as well be sisters, who lost a man who might have been an uncle to one but who was a father to them both.

The way families get made.

The way we know they do.

The way beauty is just the other side of sadness, and both things get you whipped.

Leave us be, they say, their Spanish into Marie's English, and we stand and head on down the hall, nobody leading and nobody following, all of us just a single line across and the kind of strong that being together makes us.

"We'll need to talk to find out," K says. "We'll need to find out what happened to her uncle. We'll need to find him."

"It's complicated, son," Everest says. "We'll have to be careful. Laws aren't always big enough to help those who should be helped."

"What will we do?" Wyatt says. "Next?"

"We'll give the girls time," Marie says, "to be with one another."

Now outside it has begun to snow. We watch the flakes fall from our side of the hospital lobby.

"Let's go tell Grandma Aubrey," Everest says. "And Sam."

"And Harvey," I say.

"You go," Nurse Cara says. "We'll talk tomorrow."

"Wyatt?" Joseph says, because she's turned again, she's staring down the hall.

But now she turns and comes with us—into the white flakes of cold, into the truck, down the roads.

# FORTY-SIX

THEY TOOK TWO PILLOWS.

They took three blankets.

They took both dolls.

They went out, into the snow.

They left in the night when nobody was watching.

They left, because what would you do.

One of them helping the other helping the other, vanishing, gone.

The snow had covered the snow, had covered their bootprints by the morning.

They plowed the tarmac so that Joseph could fly surveillance, but he came back with no news. On the roads Everest drove up and down and over until he reached the crushed stone that was white with snow and hard with ice, but the barn was not where the girls had gone, and there were four mourning doves, he said, singing on the rafters and a family of mice with peanut butter on their whiskers.

"I shouldn't have," Wyatt says. "We shouldn't have—"

"They asked," I say, "to be alone."

"It's freezing cold. There's snow."

"They're together."

"I know. But—I know."

Wyatt won't bake. Wyatt won't smile. She won't go to school, and Joseph doesn't make her, and K stays home too because what's fair for one person in a family is fair for the other person in the family, and K is definitely family. K is spending a lot of Skyhawk time and doesn't really want to talk, and the star has fallen off the Muni tree, and nobody has fixed it.

"If they wanted to be found," Grandma Aubrey says, "they would be . . . found. They know their world better . . . than we can ever. Know."

We're up to five blankets now and tea and cocoa. Harvey lies between us on the bed. Sometimes Grandma Aubrey sleeps, and sometimes she doesn't, and I know everything I should about oxygen now—how to feed it to her nose when she says she needs it, how to loop the clear lines behind her ears, how to watch the gauge and make tank replacements when it's necessary. Nurse Cara coming over whenever she can. To check on things, she says. To have some company. To tell me that Everest is out in the truck, and it would be nice if I made a Muni visit.

"You go," Grandma Aubrey whispers.

I go.

Wherever I am I feel bad about not being in the place that I'm not in.

And it's like this.

And it snows.

And soon it will be Christmas.

Where is the safe place for two Salvadoran girls? Where is it safe in the snow?

Where did they possibly go?

Why did we ever think, if we ever thought, that we'd be the ones who could save them?

# FORTY-SEVEN

IT'S COMING CLOSER TO CHRISTMAS, and more snow falls.

It's coming closer to the end of living for Grandma Aubrey.

Nurse Cara tells me.

I already know.

I practice missing her, but I already do.

I practice telling K the whole story of me, the name that I have, who I'm supposed to grow up to be.

I practice living without my Grandma Aubrey, but only in my dreams.

Today the snow comes on white, calm, low. There was moon at first, when the white flakes fell, and I went outside to taste its whiteness. I hung my arms out wide. I looked up into the sky. I imagined Wyatt at the Muni, and K in the Skyhawk, and the girls out there, somewhere, maybe in the safe place, maybe safe by now, my wishing and my hoping. Then the snow starts to tumble, starts to fall down fast, and I stand, and the snow tumbles on.

I never bought the lights and the wreath and the Santa. I meant to, but I couldn't.

"You being here," Grandma Aubrey says, "is gift enough."

But there are other gifts too, other hopes, and I have plans. Inside everything else, the all of this, I have decided what to do for Grandma Aubrey. I have decided how she'll live when she is dying.

I walk around to where Grandma Aubrey can see me through her open window. Trudge the big deep steps in my blue rubber boots.

Call and wave until she sees me.

Show her all the white in my hair.

"Family . . . resemblance," she says.

"Yeah," I say. "I love you."

# FORTY-EIGHT

SO MUCH SNOW, too much snow, all the way through the day before Christmas it snows and snows like the world is covering its own tracks, like nobody is supposed to see what the earth is doing. I can't wait, but I have to. I hope, because hope's what I've got. I whisper talk to Wyatt on the phone, to Everest and to Joseph and to Sam, and sometimes K will get on the phone too and tell me about the birds who've built a nest beneath his Skyhawk. I don't know if diamonds fall from the sky. But I know that the birds that could be flying would rather be down on the ground with K.

I want to be there too. Someday.

Where do people go when they are gone? Nobody knows.

Where is the safe place? Another question with no answer or none we ever found. The girls have vanished. They have left us asking.

Midnight. Two a.m. Three a.m.

The phone rings, Wyatt calling.

"We have," she says, "our all clear."

I smell the blues in her voice.

I see the smile in it. I think of Ana Celeste when she laughed her sudsy laugh and how Wyatt made her do it and how Wyatt hasn't smiled for such a long, long, long time.

Wyatt's smiling. I can hear it.

"It's happening," I say. "It's really happening."

"Yeah," she says. "It is. Best idea ever was this one of yours. Okay," she says. "I've gotta go. He'll be there in five."

I run to the front door, unlock the lock. I watch the road for Joseph's truck. Nothing comes, and then it does. He signals in and turns.

"Company coming!" I run back down the hall.

"Oh," Grandma Aubrey says. "My. I'm hardly—"

"It's Joseph," I say.

"Joseph?" she says. "Not Wyatt? At this hour?"

She's sleepy, in and out. She's awake enough to ask. She touches her hair, to see if it's all right. It looks like a dandelion, bloomed out.

"Nope," I say. "Joseph."

"With Everest? With Sam?"

"Just Joseph, Grandma Aubrey. Come for us."

We hear him out there on the porch, knocking the snow off his boots. We hear the door and his boot steps.

"Why, Joseph," Grandma Aubrey says, when he steps into the room. "Isn't it some kind of . . . weather we've had."

"Most extraordinary," he says. "Most white."

She has said her speech. It was a real long speech. She looks half inside a dream and half outside it.

"Ready?" he says, more to me than Grandma Aubrey.

"You're leaving, dear?" Grandma Aubrey asks.

"We both are. Leaving."

"I'm not—?"

"You are. Live, you said. Remember?"

Joseph bends toward her, lifts her up. She is light as one white feather.

"Gather what she needs," Joseph says to me. "Help me with the blankets."

"Am I dreaming?" Grandma Aubrey asks.

I take her hand. "You're not."

"We're leaving?"

"Blowing this popsicle stand," I say, something she used to say, when she could still walk.

We already have our hats and coats on. I've already popped a can of tuna fish for Harvey. I do what needs to be done. I kiss her. "Oh," I say, "we'll have some fun."

"Sophie?" Grandma Aubrey says, "Sophie B?"

"I'm right here," I say.

"What's happening?"

"It's a surprise," I say. "A surprise. For you."

"Shhhh."

Out of the room, down the hall, into the cold, cold air of winter.

I carry everything that I can. I stay close. I help Joseph fold her into the front seat of his truck, and then I tuck the blankets up around her neck, and I say shhhh, again, and Joseph says we have an all clear again.

"We'll be there," Joseph says, "in fifteen minutes."

"We'll be . . . where?" Grandma Aubrey says.

"Shhh," I say. "Shhh."

"Oh my," Grandma Aubrey says. "Oh, Sophie."

# FORTY-NINE

THEY HAVE THE WHEELCHAIR READY. They have the lights of the Muni on. They have decorated with everything they had or made or found, including paper snowmen. We wheel Grandma Aubrey through the side door down between the rows of the planes, past K's old Skyhawk. We wheel her in, and the old vets crawl out from beneath their planes and stand with their salute hands up, all honor to Grandma Aubrey, who has arrived at this strange hour, and they're here to greet her. They've hung garlands from hooks and ribbons from the ceiling. They've put up their signs.

WELCOME, GRANDMA AUBREY.
SENSATION INCOMPARABLE
WITH LOVE FROM THE MUNI

The door is up. Out beyond the door all of them—
Wyatt and K and Everest and Sam and Nurse Cara—
are waiting for the most-special guest, Grandma
Aubrey.

"Good goodness, Sophie," she says. "Whatever?"

"This," I say, "is living."

I push her down the tunnel of the planes between
the twinkle lights. All the way to Air Time. I point
things out as we go. The planes and the people. The
posters and the Christmas tree, where the foil star
got fixed. The PayDay bars and the pibal shelf and the
lounge where the 'Nam vets tell their stories.

"Spectacular," Grandma Aubrey says. "Just—all
for me?"

"All yours, Grandma Aubrey."

Past the rolltop desk. Past the milk-crate chairs.
Past the tools and the machines, and we don't need
clipboards.

"This," she says, and she doesn't have the words.

"This," and no joy of it escapes her.

They've laid the Air Time floater out on a bed of
swept earth and scrubbed the stains out of the skirt,
like they promised. They've hauled the basket and the
inflator, the tanks. They've checked the gauges and the

rigging. Everything like we said when we were whisper-planning. On the phone. In top secret. Planning Christmas while Grandma Aubrey was sleeping.

"Best idea," Wyatt kept saying, "ever."

Best idea because when your heart is breaking the only fix for it is making somebody out there happy.

Grandma Aubrey is dying, but she's still alive. She is still here, and so we live.

The breeze snags in the folds of Wyatt's coat.

K's hat is smashed crooked on his head.

There's the smell of something blue in the air and the smell of sky above that.

"Oh," Grandma Aubrey says. "Oh. My. You kids. You—"

She puts her hand on her heart.

"Who would . . . have—"

"Sophie's idea," Wyatt says.

Grandma Aubrey's face is almost all eyes and tube. Her eyes are full of smiling. We have our perfect timing—everything ready, the floater scrubbed pretty, the sky behaving, and when Joseph tells us to climb all aboard, it takes us a long time, but we're ready. A place for Grandma Aubrey to sit, all the medicines she needs stowed safely. A place for the rest of us to stand. The inflator fan on. The floater filling. "All aboard," Joseph says, and the balloon fills up bigger, and the rest of us climb in and glove up, except for Sam, who is bringing us the crown line.

"We're going up," Grandma Aubrey says. "Aren't we?"

"Only way to go," I say. "Only way we're going."

Wyatt hoists a picnic basket and climbs in, and K hops inside, and Everest gives Nurse Cara his white-gloved hand, and then Nurse Cara is inside. And Joseph phhhhssshes and burns, phhhhsss-hes and burns, and the white-silver-white float-er tips and wobbles and leaves the earth, and we go higher.

All I can hear is the flame. All I can feel is the sky. All I can see is my Grandma Aubrey smiling. And we are rising.

Rising. Rising. Into the silence.

Shhhh.

Phhhhsssshhh.

Go higher.

"What a world this is," Grandma Aubrey says. Her Einstein hair like halo hair, or at least that's how I see it.

We see the curves in the curve of the earth. We see the silver creeks and round tops of the silos. We see chimneys with their fingers pointing, the dark hats of the houses squishing, the plowed streets black like water running.

"Oh," Grandma Aubrey says. "My."

Over the trees and over the farms and over the cows and over the beauty and up inside the whip of it. How many miles of atmosphere? How many miles from the ground to here?

The cars are like matchbox cars getting even tinier. That truck is the size of an ant. The higher we climb we keep climbing. The picket parts of the fences look like clothespins up here, and the clothespins are just circles getting smaller, and now Joseph puts more flame into it, and we are heading higher. Grandma Aubrey's eyes say everything.

Where the breeze blows we blow, and the birds follow, squawking through the stillness sky. The blue-black birds that might look like a ribbon down below, a sash blown loose from the white-silver-white balloon.

"Will you look . . ." Grandma Aubrey says, "at that.

"I'm taking a picture," she says, "with my eyes."

We're wearing two pairs of gloves each, on Joseph's orders. We have the soft scratch of some of Grandma Aubrey's blankets pulled up to our necks. The darkness of night is headed toward dawn, and still the Santa sleighs blink on the rooftops, and the lights twinkle on the fences, and there are icicles that drip from telephone wires. Even the Muni looks bright with the glow of runway lights. It's like Gilbertine is putting on a show. There is nobody up here but us and birds and the lights Joseph hung from our own flying machine—a rule of nighttime ballooning, he said, but also, I think, our own way of decorating the skies.

"Oh," Wyatt says. "Almost forgot."

She tucks her hair behind her ears and reaches down into the basket and brings up apple Martinelli's and glasses newly shined. Passes them around.

"A toast," Everest says, "to our pilot."

"A toast," Joseph says, "to our special guest."

Nurse Cara pours a splash and helps Grandma Aubrey taste it.

"Good," she says. "Excellent."

"Yule log cake," Wyatt says next, and again she

bends down to the basket and finds a silver tray with a checkered cloth on top. She reaches again, finds a knife. Removes the cloth. A magic trick.

"Still has some heat in it," she says, cutting each slice thick and passing it around. We eat until every crumb is gone, even Grandma Aubrey, and when we're done we have nothing to say, no words for the goodness of it, the earth and the sky say it all. We are floating.

We are floating.

Joseph rubs something from his eye, and below down there is the hospital, and below us is the barn, and below us is the house where Grandma Aubrey and I live now, but soon it won't belong to us, because it won't belong to her.

Soon.

Wyatt reaches into the basket again, finds the cookies she calls blueberry chip, says she has not skimped on butter.

"Wyatt Bell," Joseph says, "you have outdone yourself."

She's wearing circles through her ears, the cross in her nose, her two pairs of gloves, her black hair to her shoulders. She leans back, near the basket edge.

She looks at us and says we are a picture, and now a bird comes, and if it could, it would sit there on her shoulder.

"I'm changing my shift," Nurse Cara says. "It's the Twenty Four for me now. Every Saturday."

"I do special delivery," Wyatt says.

"Take you up on that," says Nurse Cara.

The blueberry chips pop their juice when we chew. There are crumbs, and we toss them to the birds, and we're close to where we started.

"Another round," Joseph says, and we fly the air again.

"You think they're out there somewhere?" K says now.

"Marisol?" Everest asks. "Ana Celeste?"

"Yeah," K says, and I think about his chondrite. His best-luck charm that he gave up to them.

"You think they found their safe place?"

"I think they did," Grandma Aubrey says, "I think they . . . had to."

Nurse Cara looks down and out and across Gilbertine. She lets her blonde hair free. She reaches wipes her mouth with her double-gloved finger and reaches into her big coat pocket.

"Yes," she says. That's all she says. Then she shows

us what she has—the rhinestone shine. The pair of shoes from the doll Ana Celeste found in the abandoned barn, the doll she wouldn't give up.

"Left behind," she says.

"Well," Grandma Aubrey says. "Well."

Nurse Cara gives one shoe to Wyatt. She gives the other to Grandma Aubrey.

"Keep them in the family," she says. "Keep them for now. Until the girls come back again."

Where is their safe place? I don't know.

How can I breathe, when all I feel is love? All the flavors of it.

The clouds are gone. The stars are fading. The lights are like the Lite-Brite games Grandma Aubrey and I played when I was young. We'd punch the black paper page with the sharp colored bulbs and make our cities shine. *Welcome to Manhattan*, we'd say. *Welcome to Miami. Welcome to Seattle.*

Welcome home.

The air is thin and hard. Our lungs are making crystal clouds. Joseph, with his binoculars, says, "There she comes." The pink of the sun and its orange fringe and the purple in a curve. We are six thousand feet into the sky.

And the shadows drift.

And the chimney smoke climbs.

We are moving, but we cannot feel the breeze. We are high in the air, and it holds us.

Now Joseph leans and puts the fingers of his one hand to his ear and asks us, "Do you hear it?"

A song, coming from the tower chimes, the big stone church with its crèche turned on. Somebody is playing a song. Joseph is singing. Wyatt is singing, and Grandma Aubrey knows the words:

*In the bleak midwinter, frosty wind made moan,*
*Earth stood hard as iron, water like a stone;*
*Snow had fallen, snow on snow, snow on snow,*
*In the bleak midwinter, long ago.*

The chimes are ringing.

There's a dog in the whirl of the snow. There are the white kites of chimney smoke, and we are coming down now, and the earth is getting closer. We see the giant Lego of the Muni down below—the long rectangle roof and all the doors and Sam waiting for us and the lights beneath snow on the runway.

All of it, all of us, below.

Their home.

Our home.

Mine.

The sun rises to a horizontal splat. There is ice on the telephone wires. There is ice on the bulbs of the Christmas lights and Santa sleighs and reindeer—everything looking like it's been hit with major yellow. We are closer now, we are closer, coming in toward Wyatt's blues.

"Look," Wyatt says, and we look, and we see.

Down there. Not far. Below.

# CLOUD HOPPER
## READER'S GUIDE

# QUESTIONS FOR DISCUSSION

▶ Everyone has secrets in *Cloud Hopper*: Sophie, Wyatt, K, Marisol. Grandma Aubrey says "the biggest distance between two people is always a secret." She says that secrets are better shared. In what way do the characters come to share their secrets in this book? Does the sharing of secrets help to shrink the distances between them? Why or why not?

▶ The idea of story and storytelling is central to *Cloud Hopper*. Grandma Aubrey once says that "the meaning of life is the stories of life." And when Grandma Aubrey is in pain and Sophie is sad, she says they "both could use a story." Wyatt knows that the hopper's "story is out there . . . [and] if we find it we will understand." Sophie says that "everybody's story is the start of another person's story." She also comes to learn that "you can't fix everything with a story" and that "some stories are not yours to claim or keep." Discuss the roles that story and storytelling play in this book.

▶ Discuss your favorite story. Not just the story you like the most, but the one that carries the most special meaning for you. Why is it special to you? What makes the story yours?

▶ Everest tells K that "laws aren't always big enough to help those who should be helped." What do you think he means by that? Discuss the concepts of rules and law in *Cloud Hopper*. Who gets to break the rules and when? Why?

► Remember a time when you felt justified in breaking a rule. What was it and why did you do it? What were the consequences of your action? Was your rule-breaking worth it? Why or why not?

► Toward the end of the book, Sophie observes that "there are no good choices when you are not free." What do you think she means by that, and who is she talking about?

► Right before Ana Celeste reunites with her cousin, Sophie observes that "undocumented immigrants . . . [are] hardly different from the rest of us—all of us missing something." What do you think she means by that? What do Sophie and her friends learn about themselves by learning about the hopper's story? Why does this matter? And what do they learn about the hopper by learning about themselves? Why does this matter?

► Discuss the dichotomy of taking flight versus being grounded in *Cloud Hopper*. What benefits, real or perceived, does flying bring the characters in the book? What brings them down out of the sky and why? What do they gain or miss when they are on the ground, in the Muni, in the forest, looking out their windows, or digging in their gardens?

► The concept of family is important to *Cloud Hopper*. What do families look like in this book? How do they get formed, how do they provide meaning, and how do they help individual members to grow and evolve?

▶ Sophie is torn, throughout the book, between a desire to be with her friends and a desire to be with Grandma Aubrey. Do you think Sophie makes the right choices? Think about a time when you wished you could be in several places at once. How did you finally choose, and what would have happened if you had chosen differently?

▶ The pilots of the Muni have lived through combat, seen things that the young people might not ever be able to imagine. What about these Vietnam vets make them trustworthy? What stories do you imagine they have lived? If you were Sophie, what questions would you ask them?

▶ When the kids and the Vietnam vets enter the barn near the end of the story, they discover a "museum of leftover things." Discuss the physical objects that comprise the world of Gilbertine that Sophie and her friends inhabit and encounter. What are they and what special meanings do they have? What are the objects that hold special meaning to you?

▶ Sophie is a writer who uses language in a colorful way. For example, she uses figurative language to describe her feelings ("my worries are like the black storm in the sky that came upon the hopper"). She uses nouns as verbs ("the rain rains and the clouds cloud"). She describes the shape of K's initial anthropomorphically ("a big reaching letter, with its two strong arms and one spine"). Can you write like Sophie? Choose one of these three techniques to imitate: use a simile or metaphor to describe three or four of your emotions; write a paragraph in which you use one part of speech like another part of speech; describe your first initial as if it were a person. What is it doing?

▶ Everyone in this story wants to give another a gift—a gift of time, a gift of jam, a gift of a picnic, a gift of a surprise, a gift of attention, care, love. What do you think the most important gifts are in *Cloud Hopper*? What are the most important gifts you have received and that you've given?

▶ We don't really know what Sophie looks like, other than that she is tall, until she describes herself on page 231. The illustrator has chosen not to illustrate her. Does this matter? Why or why not? Do we need to know what someone looks like to understand their character? Describe yourself to someone who has never seen you.

*Portrait of Sophie Blanchard*
*by Italian engraver Luigi Rados, 1811.*

# ACKNOWLEDGMENTS

I discovered Sophie Blanchard in Richard Holmes's *Falling Upwards: How We Took to the Air*, found her again in Jules Verne's *Five Weeks in a Balloon*, and realized soon thereafter that there would be no going back—no looking away from this extraordinary female balloonist who, during her sixty-seven balloon ascents in all kinds of conditions, entertained and awed. She was a notorious night flyer. She slept, it has been said, in her balloon. She was celebrated by Napoleon Bonaparte and King Louis XVIII, and her death at the age of forty-one in a ballooning accident remains a cautionary tale.

Other books on ballooning and cloud hopping such as the *Balloon Flying Handbook* and *Taming the Gentle Giant* were indispensable throughout my research. A trip taken with my father and husband to the New Jersey Festival of Ballooning left me feeling as if I myself had taken to the skies; a day spent at a municipal airport at my father's side was deep, and good, research work. But it was my conversation with balloon pilot Jenn Goldbloom, whose Wonderful Whirled balloon can be found floating across southeastern Pennsylvania skies and, indeed, across the country, that kept my poetic imagination in check and helped me get more of the story right. Any residual mistakes are, of course, my own.

My extraordinary friend Matt Emmens—a chief executive officer with a sensational imagination and photographic eye—spent so much time on the phone and otherwise helping me understand the culture of municipal airports and private pilots, the soul of a flier, the glory of the land from above. This book would not exist without him.

Maria Woltjen, a Lecturer in Law and the Executive Director of the Young Center for Immigrant Children's Rights, took time out of a deeply pressured schedule at a difficult chapter in our national history to help me better understand the plight of undocumented immigrant children. I am grateful for her expertise and for her doing all she does, with her colleagues, to build bridges in a broken world.

Karen Grencik read this book many times, and every time she did she provided a new clue, an essential insight into what might make this story as important to readers as it is to me. Karen is generous, she is honest, and she is kind. She said she would find the perfect home for this book, and she did.

Speaking of that perfect home, I am full of gratitude to poets Alexis Orgera and Chad Reynolds of Penny Candy Books for their commitment to stories that reflect "the diverse realities of the world we live in" and "foster big conversations." My conversations with Alexis and Chad have been restorative, interesting, and sustaining. Alexis and Chad are remarkable people opening a new kind of door in the land of literature. They are writers who give their time to creating magic for other writers.

Through Alexis and Chad, I met Ariel Felton, the wonderful managing editor of Penny Candy Books' Penelope Editions, whose words of encouragement on this book meant so very much to me. I can only imagine what it must feel like to be a young person in Ariel's orbit at Deep Center, where she also works to help young people become positive change agents. Shannon Purdy Jones must be thanked for her kind copyediting. And Shanna Compton, who doesn't just make books unspeakably gorgeous but also makes them so much better with her careful textual reviews and deep thinking about the size and shapes of fonts, the frequency (or not) of hyphens.

To my husband, William Sulit, whose art always expands my vision, and my heart; to our son, Jeremy, who walked many a path talking about this story with me; and to my father: Thank you. You have taken my passions on as your own time and again, and I thank you and love you. To Alyson Hagy, Ruta Sepetys, Debbie Levy, e.E. Charlton-Trujillo, and Jason Poole: When I can't find a single star in the sky, you turn me toward the light.

**Beth Kephart** is the award-winning author of nearly thirty books, an award-winning adjunct teacher of nonfiction and fiction at the University of Pennsylvania, and the cofounder of Juncture Workshops. Her essays and reviews appear in numerous publications, including the *New York Times, Washington Post, Ninth Letter, North American Review,* the *Normal School, Chicago Tribune, Literary Hub,* the *Millions, Creative Nonfiction,* and *Brevity.* She has given talks on a wide range of subjects across the country, worked with young readers and writers of all ages, gave a commencement address at Radnor High, where she is a Hall of Famer, and has been twice featured in exhibits at the Philadelphia International Airport. Her novels for younger readers—*Wild Blues, This Is the Story of You, Going Over,* and *Undercover,* among them—have received multiple starred reviews and appeared on many best-of lists. Beth frequently collaborates with her husband, the artist William Sulit, on illustrated books and journals, including *Trini's Big Leap,* a Penny Candy Books picture book. More about Beth can be found at bethkephartbooks.com.